D1738914

It ain't over till it's over, baby.

THE CARMICHAEL ADDENDUM

LEXA KLINE

CHAPTER ONE

I don't know what I'm doing here. Here, in the conference room of the library, where the kids do Lego Club and Important Art movies are shown on Tuesdays and the local stitchery group meets to do their redwork, whatever that is, on Wednesday afternoon. But today the conference room is hosting none of those things, and I'm sitting toward the back of a group of people who all look as pathetic as I'm sure I do.

It's the first night of the Suddenly Single Support Group, and I'm not supposed to be here.

And there's a werewolf in the newspaper alcove who knows it.

"You new to Van Alta?"

My brain doesn't latch onto the fact that I'm being spoken to for several long seconds, and when I realize I'm being stared at I snap to attention and do that embarrassing scramble to cover for the fact that I'm socially inept and unintentionally rude.   My four year old is sprawled across my lap, whining, stretched out like a drunken cat and doing his best to add another layer of denial to the fact that this is my life.

I quickly flip the *smile like you mean it* switch and look at the person that spoke to me.

"Um...no, well sort of, I guess.   We moved here from across the bridge about three years ago.   Three and a half.   Yeah."   Quick mental math isn't my strong point and it also isn't a hill I will ever choose to die on, so I don't bother trying to get more specific than that.   The speaker is staring intently at me and nodding, a sympathetic little smile on his face while my kid increases the decibel of his whining and reaches up to smack me in the chin in the middle of a dramatic stretch.

It's a he.   Shit.   Not an entirely *bad* he either, with squinty deep set eyes that inspire thoughts every bit as blue as they are.   What a shame I'm to a point in my life where a handsome man smiling at me is about the last thing I could possibly want.   My head immediately labels him Not Bad Earnest because that look he's drowning me with is absolutely the physical manifestation of an overly earnest display of interest.   And it's way more than I want from him, so I shut him down quick.   I heft my kid up into a sitting position and hold up a warning finger when he starts to whine again.

Not Bad Earnest sits back in his seat.   I'm good at putting up walls, and he obviously knows a fireproof stone blockade when he sees one.

The werewolf in the newspaper alcove is still there when I excuse myself to slip into the ladies room.   He's watching me, his pale gaze tracking me across the room without moving his head.   He's the most interesting being I've ever laid eyes on.   I know he'll still be there when I come out again, but I'm more emotionally prepared to face him than the passel of Suddenly Singles sitting in the conference room, telling their tales of ex-marital woe and sharing sympathy over infidelities and incompatibilities and endlessly debating which is worse.   The moderator was working her way around the room and it was getting perilously close to being my turn.   I've never been above using IBS to get out of a room quickly and I wasn't about to get shy about it now.   I don't really have IBS, but it gets me out of places I don't want to be in, and god knows that's worth the mortified looks it earns me.

I can smell the werewolf through the bathroom door.

It's not an offensive smell, werewolf.   They don't smell like dogs like you would expect, it's more of a clove and coriander sort of scent that drifts lazily off of them, randomly, just detectable enough to make bystanders think maybe someone got creative with the Cozy Home Crafts Magazine Fall Edition and start looking around for the lace sachet that's no doubt hanging off a doorknob somewhere nearby.   Not a good thing, really, since werewolves are decidedly more dangerous than aromatherapy knicknacks and it's easy to assume that if you smell one you're only going to encounter the other.

I stare into the mirror for a long time.   I know that's me staring back, but it isn't a me that I'm used to seeing.   This is a different me...not a particularly new me, just sort of an alternate placeholding me.   A Suddenly Single.   A suddenly aware, a suddenly alone, a suddenly decidedly unshiny side version of the me I used to meet eyes with.   A mildly depressed and highly stressed me but me nonetheless, and that goddamn werewolf out there is just waiting for me to show any hint of recognition so he'll have an excuse.   He seems old, but if there's one thing I know about darkwalker Ancients it's that they get cranky with age.

But so do I, and my birthday was three weeks ago, and I'm to a point in my life where not only do Not Bad Earnests get stonewalled for offering sympathetic smiles, I'm far less inclined to take shit off anyone, from any realm, for any reason.   Losing my library card isn't enough of a deterrent to keep me from stomping the leg off a wooden chair from the kids' storytime section and driving it through the sternum of an immortal five feet from the Young Adults Grotto.

But the presence of my kids is. One thing I promised my husband before I shoved him with a great and brutal finality out of my life was that I'd never do business in front of the children, and though it was a promise I'm under no obligation to keep, I fully intend to do just that.

"So what do you do? Here? In Van Alta?"

Not Bad Earnest is back. He waylays me outside the bathroom as I'm exiting and I'm so close to pulling out the IBS on him again that I already have my arms clenched around my stomach - then I see the guy I've labeled Really Not Bad Bob standing about eight feet behind him, executing a surprisingly accurate yappy-jaw mockery of my new friend right before breaking into a hugely ridiculous self amused grin. Not Bad Earnest turns around to see what I'm looking at and Really Not Bad Bob - dubbed such because he spent the first half of the support group session nodding off asleep in his seat - quickly pretends to be in conversation with the group moderator.

Shit.   He's really not bad at all, and as Not Bad Earnest monopolizes my attention until the group reconvenes to the conference room to discuss the ins and outs of being Suddenly Single in the era of online dating, I remind myself that I'm not here to meet guys.   I've just un-met one and am starting the long messy process of putting my life back together in the wake of a somewhat dramatic uncoupling...picking up a replacement isn't on any of my immediate lists of to-do's.

The meeting is almost over when I lose patience with all the whining and self pity and pull the irritable bowel card again, excusing myself hurriedly under the pretense of an impending intestinal emergency.   There are a few nervous throat-clearings and at least one worried exclamation of *Oh dear* as I hand my youngest to his slightly older brother and make for the exit like things are about to go critical.   I don't care what these people think of me - I just want to get a better look at the immortal before the library's main doors lock for the night, or at the very least verify that he's left the premises.   Being locked in with a werewolf and dealing with the ensuing stupidity if he decides to go on a rampage is something I'm willing to circumvent by just about any means possible, mostly because I've got cramps.   Doing battle with premenstrual bloating is never a highly recommended activity and contrary to popular misogynistic belief, PMS doesn't make women any more capable of killing.   The desire is there, yes, but the superpowers just don't put in the appearance we're always hoping for.

I step into the hallway and duck my head into the adjoining wing.

No immortal.

"Well shit, where'd you go grandpappy?"

"Right here."

I spin around and crash into a deceptively solid chest, taking two quick steps back as eyes the color of aquamarines - the stones, not the blue-green crayon they named after them - stare hotly into my face.   I'm not armed but I reach behind my back anyway, force of habit taking over in the heat of the moment.   My hands find nothing but the back belt loop of my blue jeans to latch onto.

"I haven't seen one of your kind in ages," the immortal whispers, sweeping his gaze over me.   I know it isn't sexual, he's simply sizing me up to determine how big of a threat I am, but it still gives me a shiver that runs more hot than cold.   Geezus, why am I like this.   "I've been watching you to see if you're what I think you are."   His gaze moves to my hands as they fall to my sides, empty, and a grin pulls the corners of his lips up into a decidedly feral snarl.   "I'm guessing that's a yes."

"You're not supposed to den in mortal spaces," I hiss at him, standing my ground even though he towers over me by a good foot and a half and is leaning forward, forcing me to lean back. "You've been here all evening, you want to explain yourself?"

"Who says I'm denning? I might be reading the newspaper."

"And I might be crocheting a Scottish flag to run up the pole and confuse the locals but odds are real good I'm not."

He laughs, a snuffling sound caught somewhere between a snort and a guffaw and about as far from amused as Count Chocula from kale. Werewolves aren't convincing laughers.

"Your man Kaine, he killed Pythalion didn't he." He's sniffing me now, a rude gesture in any realm.

"He's not my man, we're not together anymore."

"No?" A microexpression suggesting surprise flickers across his face for a too brief second, but I catch enough of it to know he's interested in the consequences of two slayers splitting up. Unfortunately the consequences are all in favor of the Othersiders. If Kaine and I are no longer together, we're also no longer watching each others backs.

And I've just told this goddamn immortal that I'm on my own.

"Clarissa, you coming back?   We're about to end the meeting and break out the coffee."

The werewolf and I stand staring at each other, neither of us willing to break eye contact long enough to glance over at Not Bad Earnest as he fidgets uncomfortably at the end of the corridor, obviously thinking he's walked in on something he probably doesn't want to see.   And then the white haired giant leans forward just enough to make me lean back, effectively putting my back against the wall in a gesture of dominance that rings so many bad gongs in my alert system that it's all I can do not to reach out and shove him away from me.

And then he turns and walks away, finger gunning Not Bad Earnest as he strolls nonchalantly past him on his way out.

CHAPTER TWo

Never marry someone in the same line of work as you. That would be my advice, and I feel confident in applying it to everything ranging from accounting to construction work to slaying.   It always seems like a good idea at first, joining yourself to someone who not only knows what you are but who shares your affinity for bizarre weaponry and aversion to things with fangs.   But eventually the stress of it all weighs heavy enough to push you both into the ground, and who's going to pull you up when they're just as deep in it as you are?   In the end he and I were sending each other into increasingly unpredictable situations and setting one another up for failure, until finally one of us got hurt.

Unfortunately it was him, and with the luck of having been the unlucky one, he turned on me.

Things got messy, and then they got ugly, and then one day they'd moved into the unacceptable before either of us realized it.

We stayed together for as long as we could, but the day came when even the needs of the kids to have a double parental unit was overshadowed by our need to get the hell as far away from each other as we could.   He was leaving the slaying life by his own choice.   I made him leave me by mine.

And now I'd been away from him for all of six months when that damn immortal said his name to me.   Kaine.   It sends a jolt of palpable pain up my spine to the base of my skull, setting off a headache that I doubt has much to do with my premenstrual bullshit.   I might hate him with a more brutal loathing than I ever felt for the worst of the monsters we hunted together, but his name still hits me right in the gut when I hear it spoken.   I figure it's probably something to do with the pathetic failure I've become an integral part of.

Or maybe it *is* the premenstrual bullshit.   Either way I need to keep an eye on that damn werewolf, because once one knows your name you're done for.

Kaine isn't slaying anymore, and that makes him a target.

I shouldn't care.

But I've just doubled the size of the bullseye on his back by telling this Ancient that he's alone now, and I care about that about as much as I should.

Which is a lot.

Really Not Bad Bob looks at me when I come back in, but Not Bad Earnest is beside me and walking closer than our hour and a half old relationship should rightfully dictate.   It feels distastefully like a possessive stance and the whole idea of it puts an unpleasant metallic tang in my mouth that makes me want to spit.   Males, always thinking their mere presence is a welcome and wanted protection simply because you're female.   A quick glance around the conference room shows me no fewer than fifteen everyday household items that could be fashioned into a deadly weapon on a hairstring time budget - and a secondary glance at the males in the room shows me a grand total of zero that would have any idea what the hell I was talking about.

It's never reassuring, assessing the male presence in any given public setting.   With the exception of another slayer being present I have yet to find myself in any social situation where I'm not the most capable person in the room.   But all any of them see when they look at me is a soccer mom on the smallish side with a tan line on her ring finger and a half inch of silver roots that are more from a lack of motivation to do maintenance than a lack of time to hit the salon.

There's an almost imperceptible twitch at the corner of Really Not Bad Bob's mouth that looks like disappointment and maybe just a tiny bit of possessive jealousy when Not

Bad Earnest's hand rests momentarily on my shoulder as we cull coffee for ourselves from the refreshments table. My first impulse is to grab that hand and twist it at the wrist until he yelps, but it's been a couple of years since I've had any run ins with Othersiders and I'm stupidly out of practice, probably too slow to be impressive, and at the moment my cup of coffee is far more important to me than scaring off a harmless male.   Spilling it for this would be a damn shame.

Not Bad Earnest really isn't that bad.   By the time I'm halfway through that first cup of coffee he's looking like something that could possibly be good, if you squint a little and overlook the stray hand that keeps wandering to my shoulder as we chat.   Two swallows into the second cup I realize his eyes are a nice shade of sparkly blue and his nose turns up at the tip.   The vaguely unplaceable Midwestern accent isn't a dealbreaker either...and before I think about all the potential consequences and possible outcomes of my next actions I excuse myself, beeline for my kids, scoop up the four year old and heft him onto my hip, and flash a wink at Really Not Bad Bob on our way out the doors.

The last thing I see is Not Bad Earnest shooting him a glare that would have dropped a FaeGhoul where it stood.

Really Not Bad Bob isn't a FaeGhoul then I think to myself with a sigh of relief.   *At least there's that.*

The library, it turns out, is an ancient structure that's been torn down and rebuilt multiple times over the centuries on the same spot, a spot that a little bit of research reveals to be a notoriously thin section of the crossover line - which explains the werewolf's comfort sitting in a place where he should have been wary of human interaction. It also explains why he looks the way he does without catching the attention of any of the humans moving around him.

They can't see him. All they perceive is an older gentleman seated in the newspaper lounge, reading the Sunday Times. Not one person that looked at him that day would be able to tell you a single identifying characteristic of him if you asked them. He was there but not there.

I could see him because I'm trained to see him.

And now that I've seen him, he's making me very nervous.

Kaine is the werewolf expert. I can handle them, but they've never been either my specialty nor my preference. Too messy, too unpredictable, too bad tempered and hairtriggered. With one this old there are all kinds of complications both possible and probable, but there's no way in hell I'm going to call my ex and leave a message on his voicemail saying *there's an ancient werewolf hanging out in the public library would you mind coming to take a look?* Preferably before the next Suddenly Singles Support Group meeting, because the big guy was likely to put a crimp in what was shaping up to be the start of an interesting competition between two of the newly divorced males.

Nope. Kaine is out of the picture in all kinds of ways, I'm not about to bring him back in. I'll deal with the immortal myself, but damn if I'm not pathetically out of practice. The Purge emptied the tri-city area of pretty much all the Othersiders that were any threat to humans and the rest have either vacated the area on their own or gone quietly into hiding in the years since - but the library is letting them hide in plain sight suddenly, and I don't doubt for a second that the old wolf is just the first of many.

I'm going to have to get back into shape.

And I'm going to have to start carrying again, because fuck me if that gigantic creature breathing down the front of my blouse hadn't set me to shivering.

The worst part is that hardly any of it was from fear.

CHAPTER THREE

"He knew my name?"

Kaine is staring at me with a frown so intense it morphs his ordinarily handsome face into something nearly as frightening as some of the monsters we've hunted. I don't like it, but it isn't my problem. It's his official visitation day with the kids, and sharing space with him in my personal bubble is setting me on edge in all kinds of unpleasant ways.

"Yeah, he said you were the one who killed Pythalion."

The frown switches gears, fast - and now Kaine looks genuinely freakout-level worried. "Goddammit."

"You gonna share with the class?"

"That was Augustine. You were under a roof with one of the oldest Sainteds on the register." He rakes a hand through his hair, pausing to give it a hard tug to center himself. I've seen him do that so many times over the years and it's never once been a precursor to good news or glad tidings. "Fuck, why is he back in Van Alta? He was ordered out of this region about a century ago."

It never fails to unsettle me, the fact that Kaine has acquaintances old enough to predate birth control, the Civil War, and the fall of Rome. He's never told me how old he is himself, but as a gift-appointed demi-immortal it's likely he was born long before this millennium saw its first sunrise. I think, in the beginning, that might have been part of his allure. He was old, and beautiful, and full of knowledge of mysterious things that had the ability to scare me. I liked that, the whole being scared thing. I'd never frightened easily and prior to my seventeenth birthday I had no recollection of ever experiencing the sensation of true fear.

That was the year I met Kaine and fought my first FaeGhoul, and tasted the delicious bitter lick of being scared shitless. Standing there in the rain with black blood washing from my skin while Kaine took the swords from my hands, I was instantly addicted and already starving for more, and despite his furious misgivings he knew he had to knight me. He even let me keep the swords, which was pretty much the equivalent of an engagement ring in the twisted context of our relationship.

I was three hours into my eighteenth year when we got married.

I'd been fighting Ancients and Othersiders with him for thirty years in June.

And though the last few years have been slow and quiet after the Purge and I'm spending more time raising my kids and attending PTA meetings now than slaying abominations, that intense junkie-level need for fear has never eased off, and the familiar restlessness of the lazy fall into disuse has started taking hold.

Kaine can see it, it's in his flame blue eyes as he stares at me, his mouth half open with words he knows he needs to say but can't.

So I say them for him.

"I'm not quitting, Kaine.   Maybe you're happy in retirement, but you know I need it."

He nods, eyes cast to some nondescript place to my left, where I'm not.   He knows he's the reason for my addiction. He also knows he holds the blame for a lot of other unsavory shit in my life, and even though we'd been more than happy to part ways in the end amid shouting and violence, there's something in him that still loves me.

It's reciprocal, unfortunately.   I love him as much as I hate him, and that's the fucked up truth of us.

"Watch your back Kaine," I say with an emotionless tone I'd learned in our final years together.   "Because I'm not going to."

There's something to be said for being alone in public places.   Bits of humanity move around you, in your space but outside your bubble, going about their business while you go about yours.   Breathing the same air from the same ventilation system, sharing the same sunshine through the same window.   Hearing the same music over the same speaker in the same ceiling.

I like the loneliness of sharing a room with strangers.   I know that we'll all sit there obeying the rules of regularness, drinking our ridiculously named overpriced coffees while we scroll idly on our phones or tablets or catch up on work or write our novels on laptops plugged into the same communal internet.   Not bothering each other, just existing simultaneously in a space designated for sharing.

But throw in a disruptive variable and things change quicker than you can put your coffee down and think *Well that's not right.*   Bring a noisy child in and heads jerk up, annoyed frowns shooting on a direct trajectory toward whoever is daring to allow the disruption.   Sit an angry jilted ex boyfriend or an entitled frat boy at a nearby table and let him start in on the girl who dared to walk away from him and watch the heads start shaking in disapproval, count how long it takes for the first supporter to speak up in defense of the victim, join the rest of the patrons in thunderous applause when a barista comes out from behind the counter and decks the frat boy for laying his hands on the girl.

Suddenly everyone is not just sharing space, they're sharing life.

It's an amazing thing to watch.

And on this particular Thursday evening, it's the best entertainment I could have asked for short of a sci-fi marathon on AMC. Except the barista has a disconcertingly familiar face, and before I can slip quietly out the door with my laptop and half finished lowfat caramel macchiato, the familiar face spots me.

Really Not Bad Bob. Geezus, just what I need. A deep breath later I'm leaning against the wall next to the door instead of exiting through it, nodding in approval at him as he stands before me taking his apron off. My head flies straight to what he'd look like if that was his shirt instead of a green and white striped smock being removed from his stupidly long, lean body - and there's a short little internal struggle to keep the next words out of my mouth from mirroring my decidedly prurient thoughts.

What the hell is wrong with me lately.

"I hope you didn't just lose your job," I finally say, motioning toward the hand he's gingerly favoring. It wasn't a particularly fearsome punch, but it was enough to send the frat boy sprawling into the empty table behind him and afford the flustered girl ample opportunity to escape.

Really Not Bad Bob shakes his head, hanging the apron on the coat rack next to the door.   "He's done that shit in here before, the boss pretty much gave us standing permission to take things into our own hands if he ever escalated."

Aiden.   The badge on his chest says Aiden.   Not Bob. "Guess that was escalation."

"Yeah."   A palpable discomfort adds weight to the air between us and we look around at nothing in particular for a moment.   Aiden is cute, not in a hot dad kind of way like Not Bad Earnest, but in sort of a pleasant, non-threatening kind of laid back maybe-raised-by-old-hippies kind of way that makes me wonder if he has a pottery wheel and firing kiln in his back yard.   I decide it wouldn't be a dealbreaker if he did.   "I'm actually off the clock, I was about to leave when he came in so I stuck around in case. You wanna...I dunno, go have a drink somewhere?"

I hold up my half drunk coffee and he smiles.   It's a sarcastic little grin without any smartass words to back it up, and I find it oddly endearing.   "I hate coffee, I meant something along the lines of a top shelf whiskey," he says. "It's been sort of a week."

On any ordinary day the presence of the words *I hate coffee* in the universal lexicon of things I had to hear spoken with my own two ears would have been more than adequate excuse for me to forget this human being exists. But this isn't any ordinary day, and the tacked on qualifier *It's been sort of a week* prompts me to overlook the blasphemy dripping from that cute mouth.

"Top shelf huh?   Isn't that a little above the average pay grade for a java slinger?"

He laughs, and it's not at all an obnoxious sound.   "This is my second job," he says as he pushes the door open, stepping out ahead of me and holding it, waiting.   I listen for klaxons, sirens, the repeated dinging of a hotel reception desk bell.   Anything to tell me this is ill advised and stupid.   But all I hear is the droning roar of traffic passing us by, and eventually I go through that door.

Really Not Bad Bob - Aiden - laughs when I tell him over a glass of Lavellan that I entertained myself for the entire duration of the first half of Suddenly Singles by making bets in my head on how long it would take him to fall over and slam his skull into Carol McMickens' shoulder.   It's clear at this point that he's overworked and under-rested and is only attending the meetings because his ex wife's attorney made self-help counseling a stipulation of his visitation rights.   He has a daughter, about to turn three, and he wants to be allowed to attend her birthday in seven weeks.

A picture is flashed from a worn out wallet and the mother in me goes into a full blown squee.   She looks like him. Before he can pull it back I take a mental snapshot of his drivers license - a useful skill Kaine taught me years ago - and take note of the fact that Aiden is younger than me.

Way younger.

I wonder if he realizes it.

He pushes the worn out wallet back into the pocket of his jeans and finishes his whiskey, the clink of the glass on the bar heavy and oddly flat sounding as he puts it down and uses a fingertip to push it away.   A quick scan of the room doesn't show me anything out of the ordinary and I attribute the anomaly to the low pulsing buzz flitting around the interior of my skull.   Whiskey and I aren't good friends.   We're barely even respectable enemies. Indifferent occasional associates, maybe, with a healthy side of avoidance issues.

"Want to go to my place?"

I know he's mildly inebriated, not enough to affect his behavior but likely enough to affect his judgment.   I'm a bad idea, top to bottom, and I know he doesn't need a complication like me in his life.   I like him.   Maybe too much.

Definitely too much to splatter the weirdness of my own life all over him.

"The babysitter has to be home by midnight."

He nods and I know he believes me.

"Guess I'll see you tomorrow night then.   Suddenly Singles."

I sigh, a heavy pathetic sound of resignation and defeat that he catches and acknowledges with a hitch of an eyebrow.   But to his credit he doesn't say anything about it.   I hadn't planned on going back to that sad sorry excuse of a dating pool masquerading as a support group, but now I feel like I shouldn't leave him alone with them.

"Yeah, I'll be there."

"Can you get home?"

I dig my phone out of my overstuffed bag and make a show of checking the bus schedules.   "I'm good," I say with a smile, dropping some money on the bar to pay for my drink.   He starts to say something but I point to the swollen knuckles on his right hand before he can get the words out.   "You should get home and ice that."

He looks down, flexing his fingers stiffly, and I make my exit without another word.   I can feel his eyes on me as I go and god help me, my ass moves with just a little more showmanship than necessary or intended.

The coffee shop's lights are on when I return later that night even though it's past closing.   I stand outside looking in, searching for the presence of any discernible anomalies in the atmosphere inside the tall front windows.   Other than needing a good hosing down to wash off the street dust I can't see anything out of the ordinary about the place. Which concerns me, because the frat boy from that afternoon was definitely not right.   How, I can't begin to pinpoint...but the air had developed a vague heaviness the moment he walked in, a heaviness I had overlooked in my surprise at seeing Really Not Bad Bob - Aiden - fly out from behind the counter to deliver his well deserved smackdown.   A heaviness that was repeated at the door when he was inviting me out for drinks.

And then there was that strange hollowness in the bar, the lack of echoes and absence of carry that all sounds naturally generate.

Aiden had been in both of those places when I sensed both problems.

He was also in the library while the immortal was there.

Time to take a closer look at Mister Suddenly Single.

CHAPTER FOUR

"It's normal and common to feel inadequate after a breakup, whether it's a divorce from a longtime partner or simply a falling out with a casually significant other.   But you can't let those feelings affect your self esteem to the point where you feel you aren't worthy of love or affection. So many people fall into the self imposed role of emotional pariah once a relationship falls apart, but what you have to remember is that relationships, like all natural progressions in life, sometimes simply run their course."

I glance over at Really Not Bad Bob - who I know will probably never fully become Aiden in my head - and roll my eyes.   He wags his tongue in response.   The second meeting of the Suddenly Singles Support Group is off to a smashing start and the lavender prose of Miss Hailey Wilcox, Moderator, is about to send my fraudulent IBS into a sudden and unavoidable clinch.   I've been waiting for a jump off point for half an hour but she just keeps steadfastly not calling a break.

Not Bad Earnest is fidgeting a bit in his seat as well, and although bumping into him in the hallway and finding myself obligated to make small talk isn't marked with a priority star in my list of immediate shit to get done, I stand up anyway.   A muttered *Excuse me* garners an annoyingly sympathetic smile and nod of permission from Miss Hailey Wilcox and I cast an apologetic look around the room, pretending to be sorry for disrupting the absolutely riveting discourse on personal value and docking points off one's own tally card for inaccurately perceived failures.

It's all I can do not to head for the exit and just keep going.

Because my perceived failures are anything but inaccurate, and I have two victims to accept blame for in the blazing dumpster fire that my marriage has erupted into.

Myself and Kaine.

Not that he wasn't just as much to blame...but his part is twisted and tangled so tightly with mine that it's impossible to tell anymore what blame goes where.   And since he's pretty damn emotionally diminished at the moment, I stepped up and took it all for the both of us.

I know the second I get up that Not Bad Earnest is going to do the same - and true to the laws of predictability where eager suitors are concerned, he does just that.   I had bypassed the ladies room and headed straight for the newspaper alcove to check for the immortal, but dammit if he wasn't there...and when I turn around, cursing and stomping my foot like a petulant brat, there stands my groupmate with a smile on his Not Bad face.

"You get lost?   Restrooms are down the other hall."

"Yeah, I know, I get turned around in here.   This place is a portal shell, you know.   The turns aren't always in the same places."

The expression on his face doesn't change.   I take a step back, my left hand going instinctively to the back of my jeans where I have a blade this time, tucked into a sewn-in quick-access sheath and ready to dispatch him if he doesn't show some kind of confusion at the words I just used.   Normal humans aren't supposed to know what any of that means, and the disconcertingly unaffected look on that slightly more good looking than average face is setting everything in me on alert.   My head runs through the list of potentials while my nervous system prepares itself with a blast of adrenaline for the action it thinks I'm about to be forced to take.

FaeGhoul?   Possible.   Illusion troll?   Probably not, they usually try to be as nondescript as possible and Not Bad Earnest is just a little too pretty to fly completely under the radar.   Shifter?   Completely possible and more than a little bit probable.   Vampire maybe.   But not werewolf. Definitely not werewolf.   No clove smell.

"Is that something from your book?"

He smiles a little and it's an innocent smile, and it knocks me off balance for a second while I analyze it.   But my mouth engages to keep him busy, just like it was trained to do all those long years ago.

"My book?"   My fingers are around the hilt of the blade and I'm resisting the overwhelming urge to slide it out of its sheath and let it find a new home.   It may have been a while since I've had to shiv an Othersider in a public place but there are some things you just never forget.   He laughs a little, and it sounds sincerely amused.

"If it's a secret I swear I won't tell.   I've seen you on your laptop."   He mimics typing and I realize what he means. My fingers go through the seven stages of grief as my brain tells them to stand down.

"Oh - that.   Yeah, I'm writing a little something in my spare time."   My finger comes to my lips in a *Shhhhh* gesture and he does the same in response, indicating a complicit agreement between us with a little wink that makes me feel bad about almost gutting him.   I'm lying about the writing, but one thing you learn early on is that lying is a skill as necessary as weapon handling...and it needs to be kept just as sharp.

Aiden looks up when we return to the conference room and I'll be damned if Not Bad Earnest doesn't pull that shit with the hand on my shoulder again, just for him.   It's obvious there's some kind of unspoken competition between the two, though it seems Aiden might be an unwilling participant. He narrows his eyes and quirks up one side of his mouth in a *What is that guy's malfunction* sort of look while holding up a cup of coffee like a carrot in a rabbit trap. I beeline to it, a shameful slave to an addiction I have no desire to break.

"I want that," I moan, snatching the cup from his hand and slamming that first agonizingly hot mouthful. The scalding burn roars all the way down my throat but I can't be bothered with letting it cool. He's watching with a look of mild horror mixed with disbelieving amusement, holding the pot at the ready for an instant refill.

I realize in that clear and sharply defined moment that I could get along with Aiden really well.

It's just a shame that I suspect he's not of this world.

CHAPTER FIVE

"So why did she kick you out? What was your unforgivable sin? You dutch oven her under the sheets one too many times?"

The laugh that bursts from his throat is sudden and loud and he chokes for a second on his drink, drawing the attention of the bartender and the two women seated to his right. It takes him a minute but he coughs it out and then stares at his glass, nodding to the tender when he refills it a second later.

"Naw, I have some bad habits acquired from a wasted youth that I don't care to kick."

"Like what? I know you're not a heavy drinker, twice now I've seen you stop at two." I clink his glass with mine and throw back what's left of my whiskey. I'm pushing, but if I'm going to avoid a preemptive slay on this guy on the off chance he's something nasty, he's going to have to give me a little bit to work with.

"There are several, but I guess the one she couldn't handle after the baby came was the Arathi."

A quick search of my data banks doesn't pull up any immediate memory of that word, but to be fair I was never the knowledge repository in mine and Kaine's partnership. I was more like the secret weapon you sent in to take the enemy by surprise, because who's expecting a female with a barely-there grasp on the five foot mark and the look of a bake sale chaperone from Girl Scout Troop Five to uppercut you with a chainlink crossbow?

Kaine would know what Arathi meant.   But I don't, so I sit there staring at Aiden until he grins and brings his fingers to his lips in a gesture vaguely suggestive of smoking.

"I'm a pothead."

Oh.   Some perverse little part of me is almost disappointed it's not Sumerian for assbanging demondogs or something along those lines.   "Well, I sorta figured you for a California hippie."

"Oregon actually."

We fall into a silence, not an uncomfortable one that leaves both parties fidgeting and clearing their throats but the kind that just feels okay, like neither of you expects anything from the moment except the simple companionship of having someone sitting next to you, sharing the quiet.   It's nice, sort of comforting. Comforting is an intimate luxury that I haven't had in a long time and I feel like mourning its passing when the silence ends, broken by words that I can't bring myself to say no to.

"You want to go to my place?"

I don't *want* to say no, but I do - because the babysitter has a rule about being home by midnight, and even though I suspect she may be residing on this side of the meridian line on a slightly illegal basis, she's good with my boys and reliable childcare professionals who'll actually show up when you call at six-thirty on a Friday evening are ridiculously hard to come by.

There's just one alternative and I suggest it without engaging the part of my brain that supposedly houses common sense and wise decision making.

"No, I can't...but if you'd like to come to mine, I'll feed you leftover Dora The Explorer mac and cheese."

He dips his head, turning his empty glass on the bar.   If . he's not actually in deep thought he isn't doing a very good job of faking it.   I like that - transparency is almost like cheating, it makes my job so much easier.

He finally nods, pushing his glass away.   The high pitched swoosh sound it makes against the wood bar has the slight carry of an echo this time.   Huh.

"Dora mac and cheese?"

"Made two boxes last night and the little one fell asleep before it was on the table."

The grin that spreads across his face is pretty much the sexiest thing I've seen since my twenty-seventh birthday when Kaine took me across the boundary to a Fiergol sex club. I'm feeling distinctly unfocused when he stands up and starts pulling his coat on.

"Lead the way."

CHAPTER SIX

We fall onto the bed, groping and grabbing and rolling around like the slightly inebriated idiots we so obviously are. I'd sent the babysitter home, we'd eaten the mac and cheese, and once the kids were properly kissed goodnight and tucked in we broke out the good stuff from on top of the refrigerator and watched our inhibitions hit the floor. His hands come up to my breasts and squeeze, and it's in the shivery little moment when his thumbs rub across my nipples through my shirt that I make my decision.   I reach down between us and yank his jeans open.

The dull pop of five steel buttons releasing from their buttonholes is just about the best thing I've heard all year.

What I hear next is the worst.

There are very few things in life that can and will pull an aroused adult out of The Fuck Zone quicker and more efficiently than that godawful gagging noise a small child makes just before nausea opens the floodgates.   I've barely had time to register the gasping cry outside my bedroom door as being the precursor to something horrific before the horror manifests itself and Aiden rolls over off me quicker than I can push him off.   As if that isn't enough to send the mood to its grave, the next thing we hear is the nine year old hustling the four year old down the hall toward the bathroom, their pattering footstomps punctuated by the unmistakable splashing sounds of vomit hitting tile in what promises to be a wide arc and a long trail.

The Mood settles into its final resting place and Aiden looks at me, all kinds of questions on his face but none voicing themselves quite as loud as the one I choose to answer.

"Wait here."

He does.   I retrieve my shirt from the floor and deal with the disaster in the hallway as quickly as humanly possible, throwing dry towels over the nightmare parts and giving the baby a quick hose-off with the shower head before depositing both boys back into their beds with a dose of Pepto each and rushing back to the bedroom, where I find him right where I left him.   He raises an eyebrow and asks if everything is alright.

I climb back into the bed with a nod.   "They're good.   No fever, must have been something he ate."

"Good." Aiden watches me settle under the sheets and I can tell by the look on his face that this isn't going to happen. But I don't feel like writing off my best likelihood of getting laid in the upcoming decade this easily and slip my leg out from under the covers, pushing it into his lap to nudge the bulge that's still hanging on with a timorous tenacity I have to admire. He cocks that errant eyebrow again and gives me a sideways look.

"You know you're still dressed, right?"

It's an easily enough remedied situation and we deal with it surprisingly smoothly and efficiently considering the interruption we just suffered. My shirt hits the floor again, followed by my jeans and panties and bra, and just as Aiden is lowering his head to suck at my nipple his phone rings.

"Ignore it."

"I am."

"Unless it's about your kid, maybe you should check - "

His head comes up, a pained expression on his face that says it all. I know then that the best option is just to call the whole ill-conceived thing off and pretend it never happened. Fate and chance and dumb shitty luck are conspiring to keep us from copulating, and if there's one thing I've learned in my years of dealing with unknown variables and unlikely outcomes, it's that you don't push back when those three are working together against you.

"I'm sorry," he groans.   His caller has gone to text and whatever he's reading prompts a resigned sigh that sounds too much like defeat to be argued with.

"It's okay."   I can't help feeling like I've just been spared from a heavy consequence that, if I'm being truthful, I'm really too tired to carry.   "You seem like a gigantic boatload of bad ideas anyway."

He laughs.   He's still breathless, his chest still heaving from the foreplay that never really managed to go very far.   He obviously needs to give up the smokes but I'm not in the mood to hear a counter argument pulling my coffee addiction into the fight, so I pull the sheets up and set about finding a way to wrap them around myself without flashing anything more than a kneecap.   He swings his legs over the side of the bed and sits there for a minute with his head in his hands.

"I'm gonna just - "   One hand rakes through his long hair and he blows out a deep breath.   "I'm gonna put my pants back on and head home."

I nod even though he isn't looking at me.   "Yeah.   I have puke to clean up."

"Yeah."

"You okay to drive?"

"I didn't drink that much.   And there's something about that sound they make just before they start hurling that sobers your shit right up.   I'm good."

I can't argue with that.

CHAPTER SEVEN

The low key discomfort between myself and Aiden is so heavy I can taste it when he ascends the library steps on Monday.   The sun is just starting to drop over the skyline and he's got his hands shoved deep in the pockets of his jeans while I sit there squinting at him, the last rays of the day blinding me from both sides of his head.   It's almost like one of those haloed saint images from the ancient monk diaries and I wonder for a second if I should be taking note of the fact that he looks a decade younger than his drivers license declares.

If this one is an immortal, I'm screwed - because Kaine doesn't know him and that can only be bad news in the long run.   I stand up with a groan and give him as much of an apologetic smile as I can muster.   It's safe to say neither of us are getting over the fact any time soon that we were both naked the last time we saw each other.

"I guess you're wondering why I called you, huh?"

He shrugs, his eyes going past me to the big double glass doors behind me. "We're not at your place, so yeah, the question had passed my mind." He smiles shyly and my heart damn near melts. "You doing okay?"

"I'm good, I just..." My words trail off and my train of thought derails right along with it. Aiden is too cute, too nice, too unassuming for me not to be straight with him. I swallow hard, clear my throat, fidget where I stand, finally dragging my eyes back to his face while he stands there two steps down watching me. "I need to know which side you're from."

There's the tiniest bit of a twitch to his left eyebrow, but it's not anywhere near either guilt or concern. He simply doesn't know what I mean, and that's a relief that drags a loud *Whew* from me as I turn my back to him and reach for the doors. I can see his reflection in the highly polished glass and it's either his true form or he's a very gifted morphmage...we're close enough to the rift inside the library that he'd be having trouble holding an illusion if there was one to be held. I watch his reflection as he reaches for the door around me. The sun is going down quickly behind us, but his eyes never stray to it.

"Multnomah Falls."

"Hmm?"

"Where I'm from.   You said you wanted to know."

"Oh - yeah."   We're heading down the long corridor toward the secondary wing with the newspaper alcove our final destination, and Aiden's walking along beside me without questioning why we're here.   It's about twenty minutes till closing and the library is mostly empty, our footsteps echoing and bouncing around in the vacuum of silence that fills big spaces when people aren't inhabiting them.   I should be making small talk with him, I know, but the second this little meet and greet takes a weird turn I'll be gutting him - and I don't want to be any more attached to him than I already am if we end up turning down that particular hallway.

We round the corner into the second wing and I head for the comfy little sitting room where I first spotted the immortal, and that's when the weird turn starts.

"Looking for me?"

Aiden nearly comes out of his skin; the voice came from behind us and it isn't the one I was expecting.   A tiny little woman that I've seen behind the research desk is standing a few feet behind peering at us through ridiculously thick lenses, and when I turn around her face blanches pale in a worrisome sort of recognition.

"I think I have something for you," she says.

I don't know what I'm looking at but it seems ominous all the same, a huge heavy book with black binding and a deep mahogany cover.   Not mahogany colored - the actual *wood*, adding another couple of pounds to what I'm sure is an already cumbersome thing to move.   The little research librarian shoves it toward us on its rolling table and stands there with her hands on her hips, panting slightly.   She's adorable.   Aiden's staring at her and I'd probably feel a little twinge of jealousy if I actually wanted him for myself.   I'm relieved to realize I don't, and that's just one more thing to add to the How Marrying A Slayer Cocked Up My Life column.   Thirty years of marriage and I no longer know how to develop an emotional attachment to anyone whose name isn't Kaine Carmichael.

"Okay," I sigh, touching the book to see if it's going to have any physical reaction to me.   It just lies there, unmoving and either unable or unwilling to do anything to me, and the librarian - Marta, she said at some point - seems surprised.

"It shocked me," she says with annoyance.   "Every time I touch it, like it doesn't want me near it.   And it just appeared out of the vault downstairs, right here in the research room, and nobody checked it out. But that's not even the weirdest part."

I'm having a hard time not laughing at the dramatic whisper she's using and her accent is just making it worse, but I wait for the big reveal while Aiden is staring at some point on the far side of the room through squinted eyes. I don't see anything where he's looking, which is worrisome in a sort of dread-inducing way because I'm really looking for any excuse not to use my rusty skills on him tonight. "The weird part is that two days after it showed up in here and started not letting me touch it, I went downstairs to check the vault it was in, you know, to see if anything was messed up down there. And there was a sticky note in the place where this book was supposed to be. It had a name and a filing location number on it."

I don't even want to know, but Aiden is edging toward me like he's getting nervous and his eyes are still locked to something I'm not seeing on the far side of the room. As we're following Marta back down the hallway to the elevators I just keep thinking that he's way too uncomfortable near that rift to have come through it.

The empty spot the book should be occupying in the basement vault is still dark and new looking while the area all around it is faded with age and years of exposure to the fluorescent lights above it. I'm not seeing any sticky notes, so I give Marta a *So where is it?* look and follow her when she points toward a wall full of nothing but card files. She climbs up a four foot ladder to an ancient looking set of drawers above the rest and slides it open. "You'll have to come up here to see it, these are permanently installed."

Again I'm not sure what I'm looking at - it's an old cataloging system with hundreds of brittle old cards permanently housed in a long drawer, held in place by a rusty metal rod pierced through each card at the bottom. Some of them are taped and repaired, obviously having been removed from the drawer at some point in their long lonely lives. It takes me a second to analyze the details and start putting things together.

The card showing isn't torn or damaged in any way, obviously having never been removed from the drawer. But it holds some words in addition to the standard title line and publishing date and whatever outdated numerical ordering system it's been assigned, and those words absolutely shouldn't be on a card that old.

Carmichael, 2019, amended

"Is that you?"

The words are typed on the yellowed old card as if they've been there since it was first cataloged, god knows how many decades ago. The cold chill of dread that washes over me is dizzying. That old book has all kinds of bad vibes radiating off it and seeing my last name on the card is like finding it on a gravestone in some ancient cemetery down a country road in a place that seems oddly familiar even though you *know* you've never been there before.

I get down quick.

"How'd you know that's my name?"

"I didn't, but I've seen you in here several times and when the name appeared on that sticky note I got a strange feeling it was you, so I pulled your library card."

Huh. She's a Senser. There's no reason for her to have put that name to me based off just seeing me around the library. But I don't think it's me she's sensing so much as Kaine, the true Carmichael - I'm only one by marriage so he'd be the default in any paranormal weirdness, not me.

"The note said Carmichael and had that card's filing location written on it, right?"

She nods.

"And that card hasn't been altered in any way that you're aware of."

"Definitely not.   This is the oldest section, these are all old records that nobody has any reason to mess with.   What's on it would have to have been written on it back when this set of records was first created."

"And when was that?"

"Nearly a century ago at least.   These survived the fire in 1928 and I don't know how old they were before that."

A hundred years ago.   Someone put *this year* on a filing card one hundred years ago recording the fact that the old mahogany book was amended - this year.

My head would be spinning if it wasn't so annoyed by the irritating obtuseness of it all.

"Listen, my husband - ex husband - knows about this stuff, I'm going to send him over to take a look at it, okay?"

"I'll be here until eight, I can let him in but he'll have to come in the back entrance."

"I'll tell him."

"What did you think of the librarian?"

"Marta?"   Aiden pushes his hands into his pockets and straightens his back, and I know I'm going to hate the next words that come out of his mouth.   "She's cute.   Nice ass."

"Yeah, I saw you checking it out when she was on the ladder.   Perv."   I'm dialing Kaine as I talk and he answers his phone on the second ring.   I hold a finger up to silence Aiden.   "You're getting slow old man.   Come to the library, back entrance, right now.   Cute little research lady named Marta has something to show you."

Kaine doesn't even say anything, and the click of him hanging up tells me I've got about six minutes to get Aiden off the premises to spare him the spirit rending glare Kaine will undoubtedly use to rip his soul right out of his body when he sees him.   The old demimort has an uncanny ability to sniff out people who have touched me, and Aiden's hands, no matter how many times he's washed them since Friday night, will smell like nothing but my boobs to his finely tuned nose.

"Go home, Really Not Bad Bob," I tell him over my shoulder as I walk away from him.   "Thanks for coming."

"Hey - "

I stop and turn around to find him standing there with his hands out to his sides, looking just the right amount of confused to convince me I'm right about his innocence.   "What am I even here for?"

An instant shot of regret hits me somewhere around the general vicinity of what's left of my heart and I run through it all on fast motion, letting things fall into categories to be sorted more obsessively later.   First and foremost is the way I'm treating him as if we didn't just almost have sex three nights ago.   I'm not sure when I became such a coldhearted bitch, but he doesn't seem too broken up about it.

"I needed to see how you react to the rift."

"What rift?"

"Yeah."   He has no clue what I'm talking about and - for now at least - I think the best option is keeping the status quo as it stands, and not just concerning what I suspect is going down in the library.   "See you Friday night."

And then I walk away fast, because the man standing there staring after me with a look of absolute cluelessness plastered all over his completely inoffensive face doesn't deserve any of the hellfire that my ex husband's going to rain down on him if they overlap while I'm around.

And Kaine is coming, I can already feel him getting close.

CHAPTER EIGHT

"It's an addendum to the law."

"Law?   What law?"

"Our law."

"We have laws?   You never told me about any laws, you mean you turned me loose thirty years back without telling me there were *rules* to follow?!"   I stare at him as hard as I can, but being who he is has made him immune to angry females, myself in particular.   "Goddammit Kaine this is why I get so mad at you, you never tell me shit and it always turns out to be important!   Does everyone else know about the damn laws except me?"

He doesn't say anything, just waits for me to finish - an infuriating trait I've always allowed to rub me all kinds of wrong.   When he remains silent I know he doesn't plan to speak again until he's ready, so I sit down to wait, knowing it could be a while.

It's not long before I can't stand it anymore.

"What's it say?"

He glances up at me as if he's forgotten I'm in the room. "Short summary - it says if a Carmichael is the last slayer standing, we win."

"Win?   Win what?"

"The battle that's been going on since the first batch of creationary rejects gained autonomy and decided to be all offended that they weren't accepted into the ranks of Mankind."

I think about that for a second.   It seems fairly self explanatory.   It also makes no sense at all.   But above and beyond all the confusing unclarity it just seems sad and unfair, really...I can't begin to imagine what it would feel like to be one of the Other Kind, hated and feared and locked off away from the world that could have been theirs to share if they weren't considered monsters simply because they *were*.   It was the Frankenstein legend, only on a creation-wide scale.

Geezus.   No wonder some of them are so mean.

"That would be you then, wouldn't it?   There aren't any more Carmichaels alive in your line other than our boys."

"There's you."

"No, it wouldn't be me, I'm only in this thing by marriage. And it says last one standing, right?   You're a demimort, you'll outlive me by a long shot - "

"Not if I get killed, Clary."

His words and the way he speaks them chill me to my bones and I'm left with my mouth open mid-retort.   I suppose I've always known this was coming sooner or later, but I sidestep it anyway.   I don't have enough emotional spoons for it.

"Well, you're not going to, because you're careful. You're careful and you're smart and you know how to use every weapon ever made and a few you invented yourself. You'll be the last."

"I don't think so Clary."

There's an exhaustion hiding - not very efficiently - under his voice that sounds horrifyingly like he's given up, and I wonder if it's finally his time.   Demimorts sometimes just get tired of living, get drunk and pick a fight with something big and mean and every bit as drunk as them, finding a way out that will finally let them rest from the never ending weariness of just living on and on forever.

I don't know how old Kaine is, but I've heard him tell stories about the battle of Megiddo in the first person narrative.

And now he's telling me the Carmichael in this book is me.

I'm not ready to accept either his exit plans or my supposed destiny.

"It *isn't me*."

"What about the boys?"

"They're not slayers and they're not going to be."

"That little one - "

"Is going to be a doctor or a lawyer or a Gamestop clerk, not a dark side assassin."

"Clary…"

I shake my head to tell him nope, end of conversation, I'm not willing to listen to anything else he has to say.   I can't be the last one standing.   I'm not anywhere near good enough.   I don't *want* to be.   And by the way what in the *hell* is up with his defeatist attitude suddenly?   He's always been the most together man I've ever known, confident to the point of cockiness, talented and skilled beyond anything I've seen in my entire life.   His resignation scares me and I give him a hard punch in the shoulder.

"What happens when you're the last slayer standing and we're declared the winners?   What do we get for our trouble?"

He knows what I'm doing, but he doesn't call me out on it.

"All the Other Kind agree to cross back to their side and stay there forever, like it was meant to be from the start. No more interaction with this side.   The war ends quietly, like it began."

We both go silent, because honestly what else is there to say?   He thinks I'm the last, I think he's the last, and in the frame of the big picture we both know it doesn't matter what either of us thinks...when the time comes, destiny will decide who's left breathing.

I don't want it to be me.   I love the battle, I love the fight, I love the thrill of the chase and the adrenaline rush of the confrontation.   But I don't know how to do any of that without Kaine.

I've never done any of it alone.

When I look at him again he's gone all expressionless, but his eyes - they've got that soft warm heat that has never failed to get him into my panties no matter how pissed off I am at him.   It's so far past the narrow line of appropriateness that I go momentarily into denial about what I'm seeing.   Until he speaks, and then it's just undeniable.

"Will you come home with me Clary?   Just for tonight."

There it is.   I was afraid of this, knew it was probably coming, knew I would be sorely tempted when it did.   The Kaine in front of me isn't the Kaine I used to know and every protective motherly instinct in me is screaming to take him home and nurse him back to health somehow. To bring back the badass Kaine I married three hours after my eighteenth birthday.   The Kaine I spent thirty years of my life rounding up monsters with, the one I was so in love with that I was willing to let him teach me the skills of an assassin in a world whose shadows were creeping with the unknown when all I really should have been doing was getting my ass into a college somewhere to study art.

A bad idea all around.

"I can't," I whisper, a hand going out without my conscious permission, brushing back a wisp of that wavy black hair I loved to pull once upon a time.   "The babysitter - "

"She still refusing to work past midnight?"

"Yeah."

He shakes his head and skewers me with a sideways look, scolding as always.   "You still believe she isn't an Othersider?"

"Oh I know she is, but she's reliable and she hasn't tried to eat either of the kids yet, so no way in hell am I letting her go."

He laughs, a soft chuckle that clutches at my heart. Damn him.

"Okay.   Then take me home with you.   Just for tonight."

He looks at me *that* way, the way that tells me he knows I'll never shut him out completely.   I stare at him for what feels like an eternity, and then I nod, just once.

CHAPTER NINE

"You're late.   Again."

"I know, I know.   It's six minutes till twelve though, we're good."

Tamilla looks from me to Kaine and then at the clock, heaving an exasperated sigh on her way to the door.   It's always been her explicit unbreakable rule that I be home well before midnight and it's never crossed my mind for a second that it didn't have everything in the world to do with an inability to hold her human shape once that clock starts chiming.   I've never seen it happen, which is fortunate because I would have to dispatch her with extreme prejudice if I did.   One of those *don't ask, don't tell* type arrangements.

It works for us.

The nervous glance she casts at Kaine on her way out reminds me of the old days when just the act of walking into a room could clear a place from rat hole to rafter, Undeads and Othersiders and Immortals of all shape and size finding the quickest route to Away From Kaine Carmichael with neither question nor challenge. He was The One, the best of the worst, the undisputed deadliest of the legendary dispatchers of ancient days for as long as anyone could remember. And they all knew he'd trained me personally, so a healthy dose of respect was always tossed my way as well.

We'd only ever been disregarded as the dominant presence one single time in all our years of slaying together, during the exceptionally long bitter winter of '89 when the wall between the worlds was weakened by the longer than usual seasonal shift. I was still young and a sizable chunk of the Otherside community hadn't learned of me yet, and the waning number of slayers and hunters was giving them an unwise overestimation of their own invincibility - a haughty arrogance that emboldened a particularly large and cruel tempered landborn seaspawn to lay a tentacle on me in a decidedly disrespectful manner. It was one of the few times I ever saw Kaine lose his shit, and the hellfire that rained down on the battle site nearly took us with it.

We walked out with the sole survivors title and no Other ever looked at either of us with anything less than fearful respect or respectful contempt from that night forward.

Tamilla ducks her head as she passes him on her way out the door.

The sex with Kaine has always been good.   If I have a
memory of a single time I wasn't left panting for breath
and too emptyheaded to remember my own name, it has
long ago been buried and forgotten under too many
recollections of bedshaking orgasms and kisses that
burned clear to the bone.   There's always been a
connection between us that transcends pretty much
anything the outside world could dredge up to set in our
way, and the physical aspect of that connection had very
nearly been enough to keep us together even when the
rest began to fall away.

Neither of us had forgotten it, apparently.

He reaches out to touch my face and a year of screaming
fights fall into nothing.

He pulls me against him and all the vicious anger and
hateful degradation fade into the background.

He kisses me and I only vaguely recall the tears and
frustration and pain of rejection.

And then I feel him, hard and heavy and pressing against
me, and it all comes back to roost where it belongs.

None of it can be forgotten.   None of it *should* be forgotten.   It's done, it's history, but it's still very much there, all of it, and Kaine had done some truly horrific things to me in the end.   I was no saint, but there was little I could do to hurt him the way he hurt me, and that hadn't stopped him.

I remember crying so hard the vessels in my eyes burst till I looked like one of the ghouls we had hunted together. Sobbing until I shook with the shuddering palsy of fear and impotent outrage.   I bled for him and because of him.

I'll never forget.   And I'd be hard pressed to forgive.   I knew he'd been sick during the worst of it but my suffering was no kind of medicine to heal him.

"Just tonight, Kaine," I whisper against his stubbled cheek. "Tonight, and no more.   And don't you dare say you love me or I'll make you leave."

I feel him nod his agreement.   I don't need his words.

CHAPTER TEN

Morning pushes its too-bright fingers into my eye sockets with all the gentle warmth of a furnace firing up. Which puts me to mind of a pottery kiln, which in turn drags Aiden into my head as the first coherent thought of the day. Kaine is still asleep beside me and though I want to ask his opinion on the little bits of oddness that seem to follow my new friend without his awareness, the frown etched deeply between his eyebrows switches me into pause and rethink mode.

Poor Kaine. He'd been having problems for a long time, though honestly it felt to me like he was just too old for this life and the only way of resting that he found acceptable was to end it somehow. Maybe he was losing his mind. He'd never lost his edge as far as slaying goes, but his sudden retirement had come as a shock even to me. Depression is one thing, the black despair and violent rages he slipped headlong into were another thing entirely.

I never thought he would raise a hand to me. Not Kaine. But he became someone else, someone I didn't know, and there was nothing of him left in the blue of his eyes the night he held me down and made me scream while the boys cried from their locked room down the hall.

He knew what he'd done.   And he'd given me full custody of the boys without a fight because of it.   He wasn't okay, he never would be again, and he had no trust for himself once he realized he was indeed capable of all the things he'd always promised me he would never do.

That's not to say I was innocent in what went down between us.   I found out how capable I was of everything horrid and hateful and nasty at just about the same time he was proving his own shortcomings.

We were each others downfall, and it was a hard fall from a dizzying height that very nearly obliterated us both.

But god help me, I loved that man.

And then he came quite literally to within an inch of getting himself killed, and the trauma of facing a sudden mortality where immortality had always been a given sent him into a spiral he'd never truly crawled out of.   It had been because of me.   He and I both knew it - and the guilt had sent me running as far away from him as I could get while the raging fury of betrayal turned what was left of a once good man into something worse than the monsters he'd spent his life fighting.

And just like that, we were finally done with each other.

61

I look over at him and wonder how it all happened.   I was there, I saw it unfold around us like a book that had trapped us in its pages, each one turning while we scrambled desperately to slow the progress of the tale we didn't want to be about us.   But our names were written there in indelible ink, and all we could do was watch in sorrow as the story switched genres from passionate romance to nightmarish horror, dragging us along with it.

He opens his eyes and for a moment that deep line between his dark brows softens when he sees me.

I remember why I loved him.   And when he reaches for me, when he pulls me to him and rolls with me until I'm on my back and he's pushing urgently into me again, I remember why I never truly stopped.

"This guy in a group I go to seems like he might be a fringe Othersider of some kind, but if he is I don't think he knows it. Can you do that?   Be one without being aware of it?"

Kaine stops eating, spoon halfway between his bowl and his mouth, and stares at me like I've just told him one of the boys has sprouted a tail.

"Group?"

Not the part of the sentence I'd hoped he would focus on, so I attempt a redirect. "There's a vague energy around him that seems just a little bit off, like he's affecting the elements just by being in a room. I sensed it in a coffee shop and then in a bar, though the second time we were in the bar the thing that happened before didn't happen again - "

"You're going to coffee shops and bars with some guy?"

The edge in his voice rubs me fifty shades of wrong and I stare at him with the most neutral expression I can pull. "I'm dating."

There's a moment when I think the flicker in Kaine's eyes has the potential to flare up into a rage, but just like that it settles to a decidedly less volatile simmer. "Is that right."

I know he doesn't believe me. I'm not a dater, I never even dated him. And he's right, none of those encounters were actually *dates*, though the two bar excursions could be loosely labeled as preliminary tryouts if you squinted hard enough.

I don't know what the attempted sex would be called, but that's a part of the story I choose not to share with him and therefore it doesn't require a label just yet. The coffee pot is whistling and the interruption is more than welcome.

"Next time you're with him ask him if he knows Bartholomieu.   If he says yes - "

I wait, frozen where I stand, waiting for instructions.   Kaine shakes his head like his next words won't matter as he reaches for the newspaper.

"If he says yes don't worry about it, you're dead already."

CHAPTER ELEVEN

"Anyone want to share their feelings this evening? Any self doubt, fear, concerns about whether you're making the right choices in your journey to self realization?"

Not a hand goes up amid the sudden flurry of discreet throat clearings and the soft shoosh of butts fidgeting on wooden seats. There doesn't seem to be a lot of self realization going on in the group and in a flush of pity - for Miss Hailey Wilcox or for myself, it never did become readily evident - I shove my hand up and summarily take the floor. All eyes fly to me with the relief of a voluntary victim dispatching them of their shirked duty to take one for the team.

"Clarissa, would you like to share something with us tonight?"

"Yeah, sure." I clear my throat and take a deep breath. "I think I - "

"Would you mind standing up dear? So everyone can hear you."

I shoot Miss Hailey Wilcox, Moderator, a blank stare. There are eleven of us in the room, seated in a semicircle that affords everyone present the ability to not only hear every word spoken with exceptional clarity but each and every eyelid blinked, yawn executed, and even the occasional jerk-awake intake of breath from Aiden as he nods off yet again in chair three, without fail startling Paula Millhouse despite the fact that there's no excuse for her not to be used to it by now. But it's Miss Hailey Wilcox's party, so I stand up and smile gratefully when she clasps her hands together in approval of my obedience.

All heads turn and focus on me. Even Aiden wakes up and sits up straight to listen.

"I - "

I'm Clarissa Carmichael, I'm a monster slayer, mom of two, sometime artist though I haven't drawn anything except disapproving stares from strangers over the course of the last two years, my specialty in the kitchen is boxed mac and cheese with cartoon characters on the front of the package and there's a very high likelihood that I had sex with my ex husband last night, which was no doubt a mistake of such epic proportions it might actually eclipse the coming apocalypse as far as repercussions and the trickle-down law of consequences are concerned. Oh and I also let Aiden over there in chair three lick my nipples five nights ago but my kid threw up so technically we're still just acquaintances.

Everyone is staring, waiting for me to start.

"I think I - "

There's an interminable pause, which Miss Hailey Wilcox addresses with a soothing "Take your time dear, we're all here for you."

I rankle immediately.

First, Miss Hailey Wilcox is at least two decades younger than me and the direction of the term *Dear* aimed in my direction from the mouth of someone who's probably not even been kissed yet fires all my righteous indignation rockets. Second, I realize I just stopped caring what anyone in this group thinks of me. Not that I ever did...but there's bullshit brewing in the cosmic pot and with Kaine out of commission it's starting to look like Clarissa Carmichael, currently caffeine deprived human disaster, is gonna be the entire vanguard against it. I don't have time to care about much else.

I clear my throat again and open my mouth, and words fall out that I don't remember commissioning.

"I had sex with my ex husband last night."

A round of gasps summarily sucks all the oxygen out of the room. Miss Hailey Wilcox is shaking her head in a gently condemnatory yet helpfully sympathetic sort of way. And Aiden is staring straight at me, eyebrows up, obviously surprised and more than just a little bit hurt.

One of Kaine's drunken accusations bounces around in my head while I struggle to look anywhere but at that sweet face in seat three. *You're a shit human being, Clary.* But there's nowhere else to look unless I want to make eye contact with Not Bad Earnest, who is, oddly enough, sitting back in his chair with arms crossed across his chest, an almost smug smile settled firmly on his lips.

And so I look at Aiden and offer him a sheepish wince of apology, but I'm certain it translates more along the lines of *Yeah sorry dude, I'm kinda like that.* The accepting little nod he offers back makes me feel worse, but I have the floor and the eleven members of Sudden Single are waiting anxiously for my next words to verify that their lives, however crappy they might currently be, are nothing compared to the raging dumpster fire I'm gleefully dancing around in my bathrobe.

"Yeah, so...that. And I know it was a mistake, because he's kind of broken and I'm kind of broken and there's a reason we're not together and...I guess I sort of felt sorry for him. Blue eyes lead to bad choices, you know."

A silence fills the room when I stop speaking. No one seems to be in any rush to fill it. Aiden is staring at the floor between his feet. Not Bad Earnest is still looking at me with that unsettling smug grin. At least two of the women are still shaking their heads in an identical combo disgust-sympathy sort of way, like their heads are connected to each other across the room by an invisible bar that makes them move in tandem.   And Miss Hailey Wilcox, Moderator, seems to have lost all desire to take control of the room back.

So I sit down, waiting for her to resume the meeting and fill the big empty space that my words are still bouncing around in with words of her own, hoping to god it's getting close to break time - because if I don't get some coffee soon I'm likely to decide the whole group is comprised of ghouls and slay the entire batch of them just to make them stop staring at me.

"Well, that was brave of you to share, does anyone have any words of encouragement or consolation for Clarissa?"

If resounding silence could kill I wouldn't even have to draw my blade.

CHAPTER TWELVE

Aiden is standing at the snack table, a Mrs Fields cookie in one hand and a cup of some nondescript dark brown soda in the other. I can hear the carbonation hissing against the sides of the styrofoam cup.

"Hey."

He looks at me, a polite little smile acknowledging that I spoke to him. It doesn't come anywhere close to reaching the rest of his face and keeps a safe distance from his eyes until he turns his attention back to the plate of cookies two seconds later.

Yeah, the quick smile that disappears as fast as it appears is a sure sign. His feelings are hurt.

"Sorry."

"For what?"

"For - " I shrug my shoulder, a vague gesture meant to indicate *Earlier, that shitshow you won a free ticket to.* "I don't know why it happened."

"You don't have to explain it to me. I guess I was just there on the wrong night."

"Yeah.   But still.   Shitty way to hear it."

He shrugs and it's obvious he's trying hard to stop feeling like I did something shady to him.   And I want nothing worse than to make him believe it was just bad luck and bad timing or it absolutely would have been him.   Or him first, anyway.

"It's okay.   It's obvious you're not ready to move on yet. Probably for the best."

The part of my brain that handles damage control is scrambling so hard to come up with a contingency plan that a pain shoots through my frontal lobe and I turn away, thinking that Aiden's cologne or body wash is a bit overwhelming tonight, when my nose calls a timeout so it can run a quick analysis of what I'm actually smelling here. That's not Axe.

It's cloves and coriander.

A frantic scan of the room shows me the same eleven people plus Miss Hailey Wilcox and I stand there blinking in confusion, forgetting Aiden, tuning out his words as he starts making small talk to smooth over the ragged edges my confession left between us.

The east wall is glass from floor to ceiling on every third panel.   I close my eyes and tune everything out like Kaine taught me to do so many years ago, filtering the universe down to soft white background noise so I can pick out one sound, just one, to focus on.

It takes the space of two heartbeats to find it.

Heavy boots, a resonant deep pitched clacking with each footfall on a highly polished industrial tile floor. Echoes bouncing around the acoustics of a long hallway with no furniture to break the carry. A heartbeat, slow and unconcerned, heavier than a human's.

I open my eyes as the smell of cloves hits me hard in the olfactory gland.

Just as a large presence, tall and broad and uncompromisingly dominant in the pristine surroundings of the library corridor, passes the second glass panel and turns its head to look in at me. Our eyes lock and he smiles, not stopping, not slowing, disappearing as his steps carry him into the dead space behind the next panel.

The immortal.

" - and I'll have her on Saturday while her mom's in Paloma at some law seminar thing, so that'll be cool."

I whip my head around to stare at Aiden, blankly I'm sure based on the look he gives me back. I track his eyes as they squint and move past my face to look at something behind me. I'm about to ask if he can see the man in the corridor when he scrunches up his nose and asks, "Somebody smoking a clove cigarette in here?"

"You can smell that?"

"Yeah." He makes a gagging face and I point over my shoulder toward the glass panels.

"Can you see that guy out there?"

"The old guy with the hair?" His hands go up to either side of his head, moving in an exaggerated way that immediately makes me think of Wolverine styling his hairdo. This boy would be great at charades. "Yeah, he's gone by like three times now. Must be waiting for someone." He looks around then, leaning down to whisper conspiratorially at me. "I bet it's Marie, I can see her with a freaky man-toy."

I'd love to feel relief that he doesn't seem to be angry about my indiscretion and apparently still wants to be friends with me, at least enough to whisper behind our hands about other group members. But there's a werewolf strolling the library corridors after hours like he owns the damn place, and nobody else seems to see him except me and Aiden.

And Aiden sees him the way I see him, in his true form, unveiled.

The only partner I've ever worked with is Kaine, but since he's a bit of a basket case at the moment, a girl makes do.

"Come with me," I whisper, grabbing Aiden's arm.

CHAPTER THIRTEEN

Libraries have an ethereal weirdness to them in the full light of day, that little something just beyond a human's senses that makes them feel vaguely unsettled, though they rarely realize it.   It's what makes them religiously obey the seldom spoken but universally respected rule of quiet, reducing voices to whispers and footfalls to tiptoes and exchange warning glances with the fool who dares to drop a book.   Nobody really knows why, and it's left to the assumption that someone within the hallowed walls might be studying, reading, learning, in need of the peace that a library by its very nature affords.

It's also why the dropping of that book, a harmless and unobtrusive event in itself, booms so shockingly into every corner of the building to bounce off walls and windows and eardrums at a decibel no one thinks to question.

Nobody asks why.

Nightfall just makes it worse, but after hours there's no one to make questions a threat.

Nightfall brings with it a whole new set of preternatural unlikelihoods that libraries are only too happy to settle into and claim as their own.   And with those unlikelihoods sometimes come things that have no business using the library.

Fortunately they usually wait till closing.

Aiden follows as requested but he walks beside me instead of behind me, and this strikes me as odd.   Most humans I've dealt with tend to let the instigator lead, particularly when there's no clear indication what the hell is going on - a hangup Aiden doesn't seem to share with the rest of normal humanity.   I cast sideways glances at him as we make our way down the long corridor to the newspaper lounge, keeping our footfalls as quiet as possible.   I haven't asked him to walk lightly.   He just does it.

"So - "

"Yeah, it was a mistake, I'm sorry."

He's no longer beside me and I stop, but he's hanging back and making no move to catch up.

"It's not any of my business," he says, and where I'm convinced he should be getting mad at the humiliation of being sent home only to be replaced the very next night by someone I had announced to the group that I hate, there seems to be very little ire in him.   Just maybe a bit of justifiable hurt, which he seems to be recovering from with negligible difficulty.

"No, it's not, but I thought you should know since we - "

A hard shake of his head tells me in no uncertain terms...*do not go there.*   And I suppose I should respect that.

"What are we looking for anyway?   That guy?"   He does the hair gesture again and we resume our quiet creep of the corridor till the corner unwinds before us, inexplicably holding the Genealogy section beyond it.

"Wait, this isn't right."

"What's not?"

"This corner is supposed to go to the newspaper lounge." I look around in confusion as Aiden stands behind me, still clueless.   And cute, though this really isn't the right time for aesthetical analytics.   I never really noticed before but he's adorable in a weirdly innocuous sort of way, like there's nothing threatening about him at all, nothing extreme enough to reach into the realm of hot, he's just...nice looking.   Pleasant faced.   Pretty, sort of.   A gentle nudge would easily push him into another category but his face lacks the sharpness, the edginess, the slightly worn quality that makes mens' faces manly.

He's like a Michaelangelo with about half as many chisel strokes.   And he's standing there staring at me with earth green eyes big and innocent as a child's when a pang of regret pokes sharply at my spleen.   It wasn't like I'd kicked him out of my bed, but I hadn't asked him to stay, either.

My loss, no doubt.

I'd really like to edge up to him and step on his feet so I can reach his mouth, plant a little kiss there, see if he closes those eyes and lets his lips go soft or if he keeps them open and watches me, distrusting and suspicious of my motives. Would it matter to me which it ended up being?

I'm a little pissed with myself to realize the answer is yes.

But remorse and emotional self flagellation aren't on the menu tonight, because there's music coming from the Genealogy section…and the Genealogy section's been closed since seven o'clock.

CHAPTER FOURTEEN

"Can I help you?"

Aiden jumps and slams his knee into the back of my thigh, sending me about four feet into the open doorway against my will. I can't be bothered to have a normal reaction; all the collapsing onto the floor/rolling around/screaming/clutching at my injured leg/cursing his parentage has long since been conditioned out of me and the pain triggers my automatic override response instead.

Meaning I have a blade in my right hand quicker than his eyes can track and have shoved it right back into the back of my pants the second my brain tells me: *librarian*. My nervous system stands down and the pain of being frogged in the hamstring sets in just as quickly while the cute little woman from the other night peers at me with both sympathy and anxiety. Marta with the ridiculously thick glasses.

Aiden yelps when I slug him in the shoulder.

"Hi, yeah, we were looking for the newspaper lounge and got turned around.   Could have sworn this was the right hallway."

The look on the woman's face scans quickly through about five diverse reactions before finally settling on one best described as horrified apprehension.

She's looking past me into the Genealogy section.

"It probably was the right one when you started down it," she says in a gently exasperated stage whisper, as if there's nothing unusual about the words she's speaking.   The library has been closed to the public for more than two hours but she's still keeping her voice down as if it's filled with patrons trying to read.   I'm about to ask her if it's force of habit or something less innocuous when Aiden's eyes go to the same place hers have been staring, at some point over my left shoulder.   The music we heard is still there, but sounds like it's coming from another room somehow.

When I turn around all I see are tables full of gigantic books laying open and shelf after shelf of huge bound volumes.

I turn back around to find them both still staring, the librarian with a blank look on her face, Aiden with his mouth slightly askew.

"What?"

"You don't...see that?"

Another look shows me the same unspectacular view of a dour study area, though this time I'm paying attention and catch a slight shimmer in the air near the H row. Something's definitely up in Genealogy. I can sense it now that I'm looking for it.

But it's something of a shock that Aiden can see it.

"Describe it to me."

The pair of them look at each other and Aiden scratches the side of his neck, obviously at a loss for words. The librarian sighs and clears her throat, casting her gaze to the floor nervously.

"It's...it's..." There's a distinctly pink flush to Aiden's cheeks and he stammers for a second while I stare impatiently at him, rolling my hand in the air to encourage him to move it along. "It looks like...an orgy."

"An orgy?"

The librarian nods. "Every Wednesday and Friday."

"Okay, can you tell me what is having an orgy?"

"I'd say...about eighteen...maybe twenty..."

"Eighteen or twenty what?"

"I dunno Clarissa, I'm trying." Aiden looks flustered; I doubt he's ever been called on to count bare asses and really, anything could be on the other side of that rift. For all I know he's looking at Abominations with a testes on each side of their head where ears should be, and god knows there's not really an accurate description for that sort of weirdness. "I've never seen this kind of thing before!"

Marta is still nodding, apparently so used to this particular brand of jackassery that it doesn't even faze her anymore. "They just appear when the library closes. Nobody else seems to be aware of them but I always hear them. Sometimes I come down here to take a peek - to make sure they're staying in there and not roaming the rest of the facility. It would be hard to explain, you know? But they seem happy to stay in there."

I don't know what to say, so I just stare at the two of them while they stare past me - Marta the research librarian now shaking her head in a pained sort of mild disgust, Aiden's eyes wide and flinching every few seconds. I've seen Othersider parties before but this one must be a doozy of degenerate dimensions. Aiden finally clears his throat and looks away, discomfort shuddering off him in waves at whatever he and Marta are looking at and a half mortified grimace on his face that she's seeing the same thing he's seeing.

I'd love to stay and watch him squirm while cute little Marta clucks her tongue in disapproval and shakes her head, but we're about to be missed in the conference room. The second half of the meeting will be starting soon and the last thing I feel like dealing with right now is the round of looks I'll be getting from the rest of the class when I walk in late with Aiden trailing along behind me, potentially boned up from watching the live action porno down the hall.

"Okay, come on boy," I say, snapping my fingers to relieve the poor guy's embarrassment. "We gotta get back. Thanks for the, um, tour...I guess." Casting a glance back at row H one more time, I squint hard at the vague shimmer suspended midway between the floor and the ceiling, cursing my inability to see through the thin wall of the rift. *Not even Kaine can see these* I remind myself. *It's not a lack of skill.*

But Aiden can see it clearly, judging by his reaction. And if that doesn't make me feel weirdly warm in unmentionable areas, I'd be lying to myself.

"Hey."

I let a second pass before I look up, because I know when I do I'm going to see Not Bad Earnest standing beside me, that unnerving steely blue gaze tearing my skin off through the thick lenses of his glasses. The slightly warping effect of his prescription does nothing to diminish the intensity of his stare and I know I'm not the only one who tries to avoid having it fall on them.   Marie Trudeau elbows me from my right side and clears her throat, then scuttles off quickly with her styro cup of Diet Mountain Dew.

I turn to Not Bad Earnest.

"Hey."

"How've you been?"

"Good, good.   Yourself?"

"Not bad.   You know I was - "

"Could you excuse me for just a second?   I really need to grab Miss Hailey Wilcox before she steps out for that mid-break last-minute smoke she doesn't think we know about. Back in a sec."

His hand on my elbow stops me where I stand.

"Have I done something to creep you out?"

The urge to grab his wrist and twist it till he yelps like a puppy is nearly too strong to resist, but I manage somehow. "No, no not at all, I just...I think I'm still a little bit skittish, you know, about guy-girl type stuff at this point in my life, and it just really seems like you're always on the verge of asking me out and...I'm just not really..."

"Yeah, I know. There's not enough nights in the weekend, especially with Aiden claiming all the available slots your ex isn't filling."

I've seen creatures both human and non swallow their tongues before, and I come mighty damn close to doing it myself. Not Bad Earnest isn't fooling around anymore. I pull my arm out of his grip as discreetly as possible and turn to walk away.

The second time he grabs me I damn near come around with a left foot to his right mandible, but this is neither the time nor place so I hiss out a barely whispered *"Hands off right now or I fucking dismember you in front of all these nice but highly shockable people who don't deserve the trauma."*

He lets go, but leans in til our faces are about six inches apart. I'm close enough for his lenses to alter my vision and it makes my head spin. Boy's damn near blind.

"I really need to talk to you right now."

Something about the way he's slowly reaching across his torso with his left hand sets off an alarm in my reflex center, but it's not a violent reaction being pulled up. It's a cautious trust triggered by a familiar action, and I nod my acquiescence. I can feel Aiden watching us as we cross the conference room, Not Bad Earnest's fingertips just barely touching the small of my back as he guides me out to the hall.

The corridor is empty where we stop, a few yards from the conference room doorway.   I know something's coming - that gesture, the left hand inching slowly toward his right side, I've seen that before.   I've purposefully allowed him to walk out behind me to give him the impression he's in control, but I know exactly where he is, how many inches are between us, and that his right hand is now reaching into the right butt pocket of his jeans.

Instinct kicks in, and it's not half unimpressive considering how long it's been since I've had to go Dark Era on an Othersider's ass.   But Not Bad Earnest counters and in a flurry of finely orchestrated movements that leave me breathing a bit heavier and him smiling smugly, we end up with my left foot on his shoulder and his right hand on the back of my knee.   His left is currently clutching my throat and he wiggles his pinky, tickling my jugular.

"Did you just try to execute a Davini Maneuver on me?" he asks with more than just a tinge of amusement in his voice. He looks like he's trying not to laugh and goddammit if I'm not slightly embarrassed at my sloppy attempt to take his head off.   It might have been less awkward if he wasn't so tall.   And I need to work on my situation assessment skills, apparently.

"Yeah, I did.   Give me a break, I'm out of practice.   I've been raising kids for the last ten years."

He pats the back of my thigh before sliding my leg down off his shoulder.   It's an unacceptably intimate gesture and I'm heavily considering a second attempt while he's dismantling us, but curiosity is overriding my reawakening tendencies toward murder.   "Othersider?"

The smirky laugh as he reaches into his back pocket again rubs roughly on my already raw nerves but I let it pass, because this is shaping up to be an encounter worthy of my time.   Not Bad Earnest, the handsome but slightly overbearing accountant with the frigid wife backstory might just be all that - but he's something else too.

"So what do you do with your time these days Clarissa? Beside sleeping with your ex and playing Hufflepuff Common Room with stoner boy back there?"   He jerks his head toward the conference room.

"Have you been stalking me?"

"Yep."

"Want to tell me why?"

"We're not interested in you, Clarissa.   Well, no, let me redefine that.   We're interested in you as a side note, but the main agenda item is your ex."

I stare at him.   He hasn't flashed any ID at me yet so I'm not feeling inclined to say anything, though I suspect I know who he is.   He obviously knows what I'm thinking and finally pulls his hand out of his pocket, bringing a black leather wallet with it.

It falls open in front of my face with a flash of silver.

Yeah, he's who I thought he was.

"You want Kaine, I imagine you've got plenty of resources at your disposal for finding him."

"No, see - we don't want to *find* him. We want him to go into hiding so he *can't* be found."

"Why?"

"He's got a bullseye the size of West Virginia on his back, Clarissa. We can't lose our last best defense against what's brewing on the Other Side."

Things are brewing, Kaine's a wanted man, Agents are sneaking around watching the wrong people? Business as usual, none of it surprising. "I've got news for you, and you can report back with this and stamp my name on the witness testimony signature line if you want. Kaine's already lost and I don't think we're getting him back."

Not Bad Earnest sighs, rakes a hand through his tasteful but nondescript haircut, and I can't help but take a second to admire his dedication to fitting in with the general population. Nothing about him stands out from the crowd, except maybe the fact that he towers about a foot above it.

"That's why I need you to stay focused and alive, Clarissa. We're standing about twenty yards from the weakest spot in the Division Line and right now you're what we've got to work with."

Miss Hailey Wilcox pokes her head out of the conference room door and spots us, flashing a broad and obnoxious smile so white that we can see it clear down the hall. "We're starting back up in a minute, dears."

I roll my eyes at Not Bad Earnest and he shudders. I can't tell if it's a mocking response or if it's genuine, but in that little moment of shared revulsion at being called Dears I start to feel a bit of commonality with the guy. He turns to head back for the remainder of the meeting, jabbing a thumb over his shoulder toward the end of the corridor somewhere behind me.

"Stay out of the Genealogy section. Nothing good goes on in there."

CHAPTER FIFTEEN

"I just met an Agent."

Kaine freezes where he stands, something like abject terror flashing for one brief moment through his eyes before it's gone. He's cooking a late dinner for himself in my kitchen after settling the kids into bed and I've seen that look before - it's what I've always called his Five Second Warning. He lets whatever emotion has just hit him rip through his nervous system for a maximum of five seconds, and then he channels it into whatever bloody extremity-rending takedown his adrenal system chooses as appropriate for the situation. But there's no monster in the room with him, unless he considers me one.

It wouldn't surprise me or hurt my feelings if he did, though.

"What's an Agent doing contacting you?"

"He's in my group at the library. Pretending to be an accountant."

He laughs a little.

"They really need to get a new cover, they've been using that one since accountancy was first invented."

"And you were there, weren't you?   The very first accountant probably did your books."

He knows I'm fishing for a clue about his age.   This is a game we've played for thirty years, where I ask leading questions and he gives misleading answers.   The rules never change but we both enjoy playing anyway.

"Saint Matthew of Capernaum wasn't the first, you know."

"Agent or accountant?"

"Both."

"Damn...you telling me Jesus of Nazareth was a slayer?"

"Pretty much anyone who uses the middle name 'Of'."

I stop talking to watch as he goes about finishing his eggs. Once I figure he's thinking about something else, I chirp out "Axl of Guns 'n Roses?"

He's not plussed at all and points the spatula at me. "More likely than you'd think."

He's messing with me now, but I'm messing with him too so we do what we always do and move along.   "Do you know this one personally?   He didn't seem like an old drinking buddy, the way he talked.   Kind of formal and maybe a bit annoyed at being assigned to this job."

"What's he going by?"

"Not Bad Earnest of Suddenly Singles."

He shoots me a glare and I know he's where he always is mentally after spending more than a few minutes in my company - about one finger flex away from strangling me. "His badge said Colin Fitzpatrick but he looks more like an Earnest to me."

"That can't be good."

"The fact that his name is Colin Fitzpatrick or that he looks like an Earnest?"

Kaine's eyes are fixed on his eggs and he doesn't respond, seemingly lost in his thoughts with my presence already forgotten. I'm used to it, so my feelings aren't hurt. Not much by way of his behavior hurts my feelings anymore.

I almost wish it did. Anything would be better than the blank nothing that I feel when I'm with him now.

"I don't think I know him, but that doesn't mean he doesn't know me. Agents get recycled from time to time, he could be a secondlifer. Though I did know a Fitz once a while back."

I'm excited instantly - I've never met a secondlifer before, and something tells me Colin Fitzpatrick might be willing to tell me what it's like if I ask him the right way. The right way being a cup of coffee somewhere decidedly more private than the refreshments table at Suddenly Singles. I flinch a little at my willingness to play seductress for such a small thing, wondering when I became such a user. Probably right around the time Kaine left, flipping me the bird and wishing me good luck in my shitty new life being hunted by the world's nightmares without him to watch my back.

I'd apologize to Colin Fitzpatrick later. It was Aiden I owed penance to first.

It's three o'clock in the afternoon and the music coming from the other side of Aiden's apartment door tells me he's home, likely half unconscious in the bathtub listening to Blues Traveler. I have to bang hard because John Popper's harmonica cranked to eleven is eyetwitchingly loud. "Okay stoner boy I know you're in there, open up."

I suspect the pause that follows isn't so much him hoping I'll go away as it's him staring at the ceiling asking the gods why the hell he signed up for that group.

"If you're Clarissa, please feel free to leave quietly without A, forcing me to watch any alien orgies or B, inviting me over for sex while your kids have a stomach virus. Both of those suck huge by the way and I don't even know right now which is worse."

"Aiden, I'm sorry.   Open up, I need to talk to you."

"Why should I."

I flash a smile at the elderly woman watching me from down the hall to let her know she's not going to have to call the police.   She goes back into her apartment with a disapproving scowl and I give Aiden's door another kick once she's shut hers.   "Come on, I've got a job for you."

"Unless it involves copious amounts of either spaghetti or screwing I don't want to do it."

"I need your help, okay?   You've got in-demand skills that I'm willing to pay for."

"You paying in spaghetti or screwing?"

"Ask me again when we're done."

He opens the door and I'm right in my assumption about what he's been doing - a sloppily rolled blunt hangs out of the corner of his mouth and there's a hazy swirl of smoke around his head.   He looks like he's been asleep for three days.

"Are you going to invite me in?"

"No but I doubt that'll stop you."   He turns his back to me and wanders off.   I figure that's an implied invite since he didn't shut the door, so I step inside, my nose suddenly stinging from the illicit haze hanging everywhere at face level.

"You mad about Friday night?" The look he shoots me actually makes me finch. "Come on, was it really that bad? You copped a few good feels, I mean it wasn't *horrible* - "

"Clarissa, you fed your kids hotdogs all day and then instigated sex with me. You knew that couldn't end well."

"I'm sorry."

"Are you?"

"Yes! Look, that was my first attempt since the last time I slept with my husband and - "

He shoots me that look again.

"My last attempt *prior* to the last time I slept with my husband. Okay?" He rolls his eyes and heads for what I assume is the bedroom, and I notice for the first time that he's wearing baggy sweatpants and a tee shirt that says *Indiana Jones was a fucking thief* across the chest. I've no idea why that strikes me as funny. "So I guess what I'm trying to say is I am *really* out of practice on more than just my slaying skills and I need you to cut me some slack so we can work together without you always being pissed with me."

He comes back to the doorway and stares at me.

"What is slaying and who says we're working together?"

"It's a long story, and me, just now."

"No.   We're not working together.   You're not someone I want to work with, Clarissa."

"Why not?   You know what never mind - listen, you have that extra sight thing, you can see - "

"I don't know what I saw but I *don't* want to see any more of it."

"Aiden - "

"No."

I can't explain the reason for what happened next, hell I can barely even recall it with much clarity due to all the illicit smoke thickening the air, but if a girl were hard pressed to give a narrative it might start off something like this: I crossed the room and headrushed Aiden where he stood, grabbing his neck to pull his head down so I could kiss him.   And then his mouth opened, and my mouth opened, and tongues were doing things and hands began to act on impulses that probably weren't very well thought out - or thought out at all - and after several long breathless seconds of kissing like teenagers, Aiden started backing up.

I was disappointed for about two seconds, and then he pulled me along with him.

I suppose it being the middle of the afternoon with little to no fear of either the babysitter walking out or the kids walking in made us a little bolder, a little less inhibited, a lot more stupid.   We both knew the second we hit the bed that this was one steaming kettle of bad ideas and that it was going to start whistling its final warning any second now…but neither of us seemed to care.   Which was why when he slid his hands up under my shirt and I shoved my hands down the back of his sweatpants, we took one look at each other and started to laugh.

The sex was good.   Without the prolific use of excessively flowery prose, the closest term I care to dredge up is *earthshattering* - but whether the smoky atmosphere had anything to do with my temporary perception of a shuddering planetary event, I couldn't tell you.   What I *could* tell you is that Aiden, for being such a sweet faced hippie boy, turned out to be something of a phenomenal lover.　And by phenomenal I absolutely mean he caused the most damage conceivable with the least effort feasible.　And fifteen minutes later when it was done, when I was breathless and he was sweating and the mattress was hanging lopsided off the bed on one side, the look we exchanged said little more than *Oh hell yes.*

Round two took slightly longer, but the world beneath us rattled loosely on its foundations again when he fell to his elbows and rasped almost silently against my neck,

"You're the last thing I need, Clarissa Carmichael."

All I could do was agree with him.

CHAPTER SIXTEEN

"So we're like...friends with benefits?"

A moment's consideration culminated in nothing more than a halfhearted shrug. "Yeah, I guess. I benefit from your ability to see through walls and you benefit from my willingness to make extra spaghetti on Wednesdays."

"That's not really the benefit I was referring to."

I watch while he hefts the mattress back into a halfhearted semblance of straightness on the box spring. "Well...I sorta thought we'd leave that one unsaid and heavily inferred."

"Heavily inferred," he repeats, tasting each of the words individually and then saying them again together. A little nod combined with a quirk to the right side of his mouth seems like as close to agreement as he plans to come on the subject. "So I don't suppose we walk into Suddenly Singles on Friday night holding hands."

"Ah...uh, no. No, we don't do that. Unless you want Not Bad Earnest giving you *that look*."

"Not Bad Earnest?"

"My pet name for Colin Fitzwhatever."

"You gave us all names?" His head cocks to one side and my eyes, I swear, go half moony. He's too damn cute and the not so distant memory of that sweet face dripping with the sweat of full-fuck exertion with his long dark hair falling over his eyes is sending a shiver directly to all points south. "Who am I?"

"Hm?"

"Your pet name for me."

"Oh." I notice his sweats are riding so low on his hips that the deep little dimples just above his butt are all exposed and in desperate need of kissing. "I told you this. You're Really Not Bad Bob."

He quirks a brow. *Oh no. No, don't do that.* He's got that shiny dark hair, almost as dark as Kaine's but long enough to brush his shoulders…dark brows that furrow in the middle, not near as deep as Kaine's but definitely reminiscent of Mister Carmichael circa thirty years ago, and I'm suddenly having hormonal pain.

Don't go there. Aiden is nothing like Kaine, you just like tall dark haired men. There's nothing creepy about that.

"Bob?"

"Yeah, you fall asleep ten minutes into the meeting and your head bobs while you're dozing." I do a quick impression of it. "It's pretty funny, we take bets on how long till your forehead hits your knees."

The little laugh that bubbles from his throat makes me groan, and it's a sound of desperation and resignation and a shameful and absolute failure to resist the pull of a sweet face and long legs and narrow hips and the goddamn way he moaned against my ear and asked for permission in a breathless whisper right before he let go and came inside me.

I'm so damn weak.

But I know there are plenty more condoms in the bedside table, and Kaine has the kids today.

*Bless your cranky ass, Kaine Carmichael...*if there's one thing he always comes through for me on it's being a good father to our kids, and that's just about to come in handy.

I only feel a little bit weird that he's in my head as Aiden flops down on the bed, patting the newly repositioned mattress beside himself in an open invitation for me to come occupy it. And as I do just that, I shoo Kaine out and shut the door behind him. My head doesn't belong to him anymore, just like my heart doesn't, my soul doesn't, my body doesn't. All the things I gave him so freely at such a tender young age, all the things he'd earned and fought for and promised me he would keep forever - they all belong to me again now, and it's an odd feeling.

None of me is his. Not now. Likely not ever again.

I'd probably be sad if Aiden wasn't tugging me over onto his chest and smiling at me like he's just had his first lay and is looking forward to his second.

"I remember you saying I was the last thing you needed, hippie boy."

"I said that. Yes, I did. And I meant it."

I'm set to get my feelings hurt just a tiny bit when he reaches over to the bedside table to pluck a smoldering joint from the coffee cup that's been doubling for an ashtray. He waves it under my nose with a wicked little grin that takes that sweet face to a whole new level of nauseatingly adorable before he takes a drag off it, and I watch with a delightfully dizzy head as he returns it to the cup and brings his attention back to me.

"You're the last thing I need...but god help my sorry ass, I want you."

CHAPTER SEVENTEEN

"Left hand, Clary."

It's three weeks later, three weeks since I first slept with Aiden, and against my better judgement I've had him in my bed at least six times since then. Something tells me Kaine is aware of this and there's been an unsettling formality between us ever since. The good part of this uncomfortable situation is that he hasn't tried to bed me again himself, and though the shitty side of my female vanity wants to be all pouty about that little fact, my sensible side knows it's the best scenario for both of us.

No more sex between me and Kaine. But there's a tension there, the same tension that's always fired us up and kept us tearing at each other either physically or intellectually, and now it's channeling itself into something far more productive than orgasms and arguments.

He's been retraining me. Everything he ever taught me is coming back online, some of it quick and easy like muscle memory and the simple reactionary impulse of a body conditioned so deeply that it acts on its own without being told by the brain - and some of it not so easy, not so quick, and definitely not so painless.

Kaine's never been an easy teacher. Aiden has stopped questioning my bruises, accepting my insistence that it's a side effect of the monster-slaying version of Krav Maga and not an abusive ex beating the shit out of me.

Though there's not much difference, to be honest.

He tells me the end is coming and that I'm likely this side's last line of defense. Funny, how Not Bad Earnest said those very same words in reference to *him* not so terribly long ago. I've stopped questioning him about where he plans to be when this impending apocalypse touches down and why no other slayers seem to be appearing to lend a hand.

It's going to be you, he tells me.

Not what I want to hear.

"I said *left hand.*"

"NO."   I put my arms down and turn to walk away, but he isn't going to let me leave and I know it.

"What did you say?"

"I said no.   I'm not doing the reverse attack stance, I don't like it, I'm not any good at it.   It's pointless."

The murderous rage in his face doesn't even set me on alert, I'm so tired and cranky and sore.   And I'm not even remotely listening when he starts to light into me for the third time about why all this is so important in the first place.

"Clary, the divider is weakening - when it fails we're going to have all of mankind's worst nightmares flooding into this world.   And when they do, you're going to need to cross over to their side and take out whoever's leading them. They're an authority based community, without a strong head the body will collapse."

"I have a better idea, why don't *you* do that."

"Because it's not my fight.   Not anymore."

"You're just going to sit this one out?"

"Damn straight.   And you're going to have to function in flipside over there, so do the reverse attack stance and start liking it."

I don't know what makes me drop my dagger and walk away, but I do know it's a bad idea all around.   But I've been all about bad ideas lately and even being in the same room with Kaine falls solidly into that category, so it really isn't surprising when he comes up behind me and grabs me.   I know it's coming - I'm hard to sneak up on and he isn't making any effort to be covert - and when he grips my face with one big hand and yanks my head to the side, I snap.

Which, in the end, I'm pretty sure was his intention.

"You listen to me Clary, the world is going to *end*, do you understand what that means?   It means you, me, the boys, that pretty stoner you've been fucking, all of it *gone*, forever - do you understand me? *Gone*, Clary." He lets go and takes a step back, leaving me seething with a rage that's been boiling inside me since a full year before I kicked his ass out of the house.

That was his second mistake, letting go - his first was touching me in the first place. And though hindsight tells me he anticipated every single reaction his actions pulled from me, I'd like to spend at least a few seconds believing I actually had one up on him when I came around and snatched the dagger from his belt.

The calm look on his face makes it clear this is just another level of the training session, just like when I was seventeen and he shoved me over the top rail of the McTier Street bridge and told me he was going to do one of two things if I was lucky, both if I wasn't. I'd arrogantly asked what the two things were, hanging there with my top half dangling over the black water two stories down, anchored only by his grip on the back of my blue jeans. I remembered it vividly.

It was the first time I'd ever felt horny during a clinch situation.

Kaine wasn't amused, of course. I was young and stupid and didn't have the built in combination of common sense and fear of the unknown that kept most people alive till they met their deaths by natural causes...but there was nothing natural about what we were up against, and my lack of a panic button was his best weapon.

A year later when I was old enough, he'd taken me back to McTier and showed me the two things, both of which resulted in me getting wet...but only one ending up with me in the water.

All that plays in my head while I stand there holding his own dagger in his face, running a quick systems check to see if I can guess where his other blade is going to get me the moment I make my move. I can't feel the sharp tip poking me anywhere, but that doesn't mean it isn't already drawing blood.

"Do you really want to play games Clary?"

"I told you I'm doing this my way, since you're too big of a pussy to help you *don't* get to give me orders." My heel comes down on his left foot, which doesn't bring much of a response, but when I put all my weight on it and pull him forward he loses his balance and we both go down. It's a stupid, messy, ineffective move on my part - but in his scramble to keep from falling on me, he throws both hands out on either side of my head.

Including the hand holding the knife.

Which makes me the only one armed in any meaningful way.

"You were saying?"

There's an *Oh hell no* moment when I think he's going to kiss me, when his eyes drift down to my mouth and I have to assess exactly how devoted I am to abstinence where he's concerned and my brain shifts into a play by play of the seventeen ways he's taught me to get an unwelcome body off of your own.   The first option I speed toward is the universal default of a swift knee to the groin, but Kaine isn't kissing me, and the knife in my hand isn't making anything close to a meaningful dent in the side of his neck.

His eyes come back to mine and I feel that old familiar pain in my gut.   He's always been the most beautiful man I ever saw in my life...and those silvery blue eyes are still as bright and full of fire as they were the day I first met him, despite how old I know he has to be now.   But there's a fatigue lurking behind them that tells me to look hard, because one of these days will be the last time I ever get to stare into them.

I'm not sure I'm ready for that.

"Tell me, Kaine."

He sighs and gets up on his knees, looking down at me as he slides his blade back into his belt.   He knows what I want to hear.   And I know he has no intention of telling me, not today, not tomorrow.   Not ever.

"You don't want to know, Clary."

Something in his voice tells me he means more than just his age...there's something else I don't want to know besides simply how old he is, though to be honest a number would be enough for me and he could keep the rest.   I've been after this piece of information for thirty years and for thirty years he's smirked at me and shook his head every time I badger him about it.   His steadfast refusal to give me an answer - or even a hint - has been a hallmark of our relationship from day one.

And it looks like it's going to stay that way.

I have a secret of my own though, and the difference between his and mine is that I'm anxious to spill.

"Remember McTier?"

He holds his hand down to me and I take it, letting him pull me up off the floor.   There's a little grin on his face and I know his memories of that part of our life together are just as precious to him as they are to me regardless of where we are now.   We were so improbable...but so damn *excited* to be together, doing what we were doing, for however long we managed to stay alive doing it.

"We spent our first night together making love on top of that bridge."

"Yeah.   That was where you told me I wasn't going to grow anymore."

"You were mad at me for that."

"Of course I was - I wanted to be tall and imposing and then you told me I'd already topped out and was going to be five-two for the rest of my life. You've always been the bearer of bad tidings, Kaine."

He's laying his blades on the table neatly, meticulously, the way he always does. I notice there are two more than I'd been aware of during our tussle and wonder when he'd gotten soft enough to refrain from pulling either of them on me. "Yeah. Sorry. But the rest of it was good, eh?"

"Losing my virginity in a rain storm on top of a heavily traveled thoroughfare while buses passed underneath? Excellent."

He pulls another blade from the back of his pants and inspects the edge. "I kept you dry. Well...the parts of you that didn't need to be wet."

"Oh ho."

Don't listen to him I remind myself. *He's always known how to get you naked without laying a hand on you. Buck up or back up.*

Now's the time.

"Do you remember when I asked you how a person knows they're finished?"

A raised eyebrow tells me that yes, he remembers, and yes, he senses this is going somewhere he may not want to follow...but I've been following him everywhere he's led me for the last three decades and it's time for him to listen to me. I have one simple truth that needs to be revealed.

I don't want to do this anymore.

It's a sudden choice, maybe a kneejerk one that hasn't been terribly well thought out and is based more on emotional factors than hardline fact - but it's the *right* one and I know that none of it, not the slaying or the whole fending off of the apocalypse or the last man standing scenario, not one bit of it is going to end well for me without Kaine. I wasn't sure - *really* sure - until he told me I was it, that I was going to do it alone, and when it came to me it came with a solid sureness strapped onto its back that I had no desire to second guess.

There are so many factors twisted up in this decision, and amazingly they're not even entirely selfish. Because every time I think about the fact that I've recruited an innocent, inexperienced, ridiculously young guy with a huge future ahead of him to back me up in the shitstorm that's coming, my head goes straight to the picture in his wallet of the little dark haired baby girl that looks exactly like him, and how he just went to her third birthday party the day after I put a dagger in his hand and showed him where the major organs are on various Othersider creatures in comparison to our own. And that takes me straight to a flash forward that never ends well. I don't have any particular gift of foresight, but it doesn't take spooky skills to close your eyes and see all the different kinds of blood that can spatter across a floor, and how they look mixed with human.

And then there's me, with all my flaws and failings, still wanting very much to stay alive despite it all. I have kids to finish raising and a new life to start living…and I've decided I'm done. I came into this training session intending to see it through, but now, halfway into the lesson, I know there's only one reason to continue.

Homefront protection is my only goal now. Hunting, going out in pursuit of the battle, that's an occupation I'm walking away from as of this very moment as Kaine stands staring at me, waiting for me to say it.

To be honest I know I'm going to miss it bitterly. The excitement of it all has been my drug of choice, and I'm a happy addict. But the last ten years of my life have been spent guiding two boys toward hopefully the right path in life while settling begrudgingly into the whole suburban housewife thing, and it hasn't been altogether unpleasant. Boring at times, yes. Occasionally mind-numbing and unfulfilling, yeah, no argument there. But my boys have taken up the spaces that semi retirement had left empty, and though nothing in the world can match the thrill of what I spent all those years doing with Kaine, I'm fairly certain I can find a niche in the real world to eventually be comfortable in without him. I know I told him not long ago that I wasn't quitting regardless of what he chose to do himself. I'm taking that back now.

I've let him retrain me because I know things aren't safe and I need to be able to defend myself and our boys, but that's the extent of why I've agreed to it.   I won't be using it to march across the dividing line and take out the boss that's standing between this world and that one.   I won't be fighting an army of abominations and I won't be heading off any worldwide takeover.

Once upon a time, maybe...with Kaine.   But I know I can't do any of it without him and it would be stupid and foolhardy for me to try.   He's the demi immortal...I'm just Clarissa, mom of two, mortal human idiot with an adrenaline addiction that I really need to kick before it's too late.

It's time to tell him.

"You said there's a sense of relief, and completion, and then you don't want to do it anymore.   That's where I am in life, Kaine.   That quote's not just about orgasms anymore, it's life.   *This* life."

He shakes his head, and I know it's the pained denial of a man who feels like he's failed at something very important.

"You have a job to do, girl.   You know how it has to be."

"I know how it was *supposed* to be.   I know you were supposed to be doing this with me beside you, that it was supposed to be you in charge and I was supposed to be Robin to your Batman.   But you walked away, so now I am too.   I have to."   He's still shaking his head, so I go shamelessly for the big guns.   "I don't want to die before our kids are grown and can fend for themselves."

The mention of our children changes something in his face, and after a long moment of pained silence his determined headshake switches to a weary nod of acceptance.

And then he pulls out a big gun of his own.

"We were good, Clary."

I sigh, not because I know what's coming, but because I know what's already passed.

"Not good enough apparently."

I don't remember giving Kaine any indication that I was okay with physical contact apart from beating the shit out of each other in hand to hand combat, but that doesn't stop him from reaching out and sliding a big hand around my waist.

"We can try again, Clary."

I've no active memory of exactly when I turned the corner from broken quitter to self motivated feminist, but right at this moment being Kaine's reclaimed conquest fills me with so much anger and disgust that I grab his fingers and bend them back as hard as I can.   His reflexes kick in and he has me spun around and yanked back against him quicker than I can crank his fingers again.   The lack of a satisfying crack telling me I've broken at least one of his bones just stokes my anger to a tidy little flareup and I lay viciously into the top of his foot with my boot heel.   The grunt from the broad chest behind me sends a momentary signal that he's probably done, but maybe two seconds later I find myself flat on my back on the floor with him sitting on my stomach, wondering how the hell I let him do this to me for the ten thousandth time in our mutual history.   And if that doesn't just fill me with the most violent rage I've ever felt in my life, all I can say is I'm either delusional or lying through my teeth.

Because as I look up into his icy blue eyes and see them sweeping down my chest, I suddenly want to kill him.   Not because I'm mad at him or frustrated because he's used his superior size and strength to best me yet again.

No.

It's because the last time we were in this position he'd forced me to do something I didn't want to do, and I'm way past being traumatized by the memory of being powerless under him.   Now I'm solidly in the realm of blind rage at feeling it again.   But this time I'm not completely without resources and as I bring my left leg up and slam the back of my boot heel down into his kidney, my hand goes under my back and my fingers wrap around the ridged hilt of a backup knife of my own.

Ten years ago this amateur move wouldn't have done more than make Kaine slam my head into the floor. Just two years ago it would have done little more than aggravate him into twisting my arm up behind me till it snapped at the elbow. A year ago maybe it would have provoked him into cracking me in the skull with his own forehead.

But now...now he gasps, a sharp intake of breath that tells me I've hurt him, and I feel his body go rigid with centuries of training that can't be shocked out of him by his bladder suddenly filling with blood. Any other man would have gone limp, but this is a slayer, a demimort, a man who was created for the specific purpose of being a badass long enough to outlive the bad guys. But even though his body is still on alert, I can tell that his mind is reeling with the pain I've inflicted.

It's then that I realize Kaine is getting *really* old.

He lays on top of me for a few seconds, the rage gone out of him and me both. The need to fight is filtered through a sieve of physical agony for him and emotional turmoil for me; the urge to flip him over onto his back and immediately tend to him is so strong I have to give myself an internal chastising to keep from cradling him in my arms until that look of pain is gone from his face.

I'm so mad at myself.   Not for hurting him…he's a grown ass man, he can take care of himself.   He's an ancient, damn near indestructible, the toughest man I've ever met in my entire lifetime of experiences with exceptionally tough beings of both the man and monster varieties.   I've seen him take an axe between the shoulder blades and simply reach back over his head to pull it out and swing it at the attacker closest to him without so much as wincing. No, I don't feel bad about the fact that he'll be pissing blood in the morning.

I feel bad that I didn't listen to him.

Because Kaine's been telling me for a couple of years now that he's tired, he doesn't want to do it anymore, that his slayer days are coming to a close and that it's going to be up to me if things go sideways later down the road.   He's hinted heavily that he's ready to just stop *being*…it's the malady that eventually gets into the soul of every ancient, the end of their will to keep living.   And I've just been telling him to stop being a drama queen, to suck it up and do his damn job.

Now here he is, struggling to level his breathing, focusing on the pain for the first time probably in his entire life.

It's a terrifying thing to see.

"Kaine - "

He rolls over off me and flops onto his back on the floor next to me.   It's an ungraceful move and that disturbs me, because Kaine has always moved with the smooth agility of a cat and now he seems so...messy. It could be because I just deflated his left kidney, but I really doubt it.

"Why did you stop?"

"What?"

"You should have put that blade in my back. Why didn't you?" He's scolding me, telling me I should have, not truly wondering why I didn't. I sit up and shove his leg off me where it's laying across my knees.

"If you're hoping I'll put you out of your misery it's going to be a long wait, old man. I'm not up for doing you any favors." I realize I'm still mad about being pinned down and the memories it dredged up, but that's not a subject I want to rehash with him again. The last time it came up he apologized and I ended up sleeping with him, a mistake I won't be repeating.

I have history with him. I have children with him. I have thirty years of one hell of a wild ride with him.

What I don't have is the strength to stay with him through what will probably be a miserable final few years before he finds some spectacular way to burn out. I would rather it all end with me hating him than pitying him, because creatures like Kaine Carmichael have no capacity for accepting pity.

And to be honest, I don't have a lot of it left to give.

CHAPTER EIGHTEEN

I'm hung over the next morning, cranky and sick and not in the mood for doorbells that result in doors opening to reveal tall, thin, slightly hippie-ish sidekicks-slash-friends-with-benefits bearing Starbucks and sheepish grins.   My training session with Kaine and the subsequent revelation that he was on his last legs metaphorically speaking had sent me careening into a half bottle of Scottish whiskey and a whole lot of self loathing.

No metaphors involved in that part.

"Aiden, I'm in no mood - "   I take the coffee from his hand and start to shut the door, but he steps quickly inside before I can get it closed.

"Listen," he starts despite the clear warning on my face. "I've been looking into the lay of the land that the library sits on and there's some weird stuff."   I watch as he pulls a big roll of papers out of his backpack, knowing the entire scenario that's about to play out is one hundred percent my own doing.   I've spent the last three weeks talking to him even more than I've been sleeping with him, explaining to him what Kaine is by default and what I am by choice, and instead of eyerolling disbelief I've been met with the excited exuberance of a labrador puppy with an uncanny skill for research and an anxious desire to be put to work. Aiden has embraced the whole whack story like it's a new chapter of the gospel, and though I'm relieved he's not waving goodbye with his middle finger up, I'm not particularly thrilled to be sprayed with his eagerness on this particular morning while my head feels like it's stuck in a perpetually flushing toilet. "It's all really old records but according to the land surveys and geological reports, there's a fault that runs right under the hills on the east side of the city. The library was built smack on top of it."

He stops talking suddenly and I groan into my caramel macchiato. I know Kaine has just come out of the bedroom behind me and that he's wearing nothing but his boxers. I also know that nothing happened between us after I relocated one of his internal organs other than a few shots of fairly decent whiskey followed by two firmly shut bedroom doors. I slept with the boys, he took the big bed so he could stretch out and let his regenerative stuff do its tricks without shoving me onto the floor in the middle of the night.

Aiden doesn't know any of this though, and the look on his face as he stuffs his papers back into his pack and turns to reach for the doorknob is just one small step from heartbreaking.

"I'll come back later."

I should stop him, I know - follow him out into the driveway, assure him that Kaine was too sick to go home and I drank until I passed out in my kids' room and nothing went on other than the youngest complaining about my snoring while the oldest counted how many times he heard his daddy throw up across the hall.   But for some reason I don't do it.   I've been feeling contrary ever since Kaine pinned me and Aiden has the sorry misfortune of being of the same gender as the man I'm mad at, and I don't owe any of them anything.

You're a shit human being, Clary.

Aiden doesn't look at me as he closes the door behind him.

I should feel bad, but all I feel is tired.

Bad can wait.

Aiden meets me at the library on Monday.   He doesn't want to come to my house anymore and I can't say I blame him;   I'm not sure he trusts me now, but his enthusiasm for the job hasn't been diminished by what I'm sure he considers a betrayal of a particularly painful kind. Seeing Kaine in my kitchen that early in the morning has to have been a blow to a guy who just two nights previous had lain in bed with me straddling his hips, gazing up into my face with something like a bright eyed adoration while telling me we should drop out of Suddenly Singles and start spending our Friday nights in bed together.

Yeah, I wouldn't trust me either.

"Nothing happened between me and Kaine the other night. In case you...you know...thought it had."

He shrugs, and it's like that night weeks ago when I spewed my confession about bedding my ex to the entire group. He'd tried so hard to let it roll off his shoulders, but the hurt had been shockingly bright in his eyes even though the rest of his face said it was no biggie.

And that was before there was anything between us.

The ugly truth of it was that I had no idea what I was doing. I'd unhitched my wagon from Kaine's horse and was drifting half blind in a snowstorm without a compass across a wide open wilderness of uncharted territory, without any idea which direction I should be headed and stumbling off every cliff that dropped in front of me.

Aiden was one of those cliffs.

And so was Kaine.

And I just kept tripping over both of them.

"I'm a big boy, Clarissa. You don't have to babysit my feelings."

There's probably a hundred things I know I should say, but I can't for the life of me think of the words to put together even one of them. So I do the absolute worst thing I could possibly do and open my mouth anyway.

"I've been with Kaine for most of my life."

Aiden flinches, but I keep going. "I married him when I was eighteen. Like, *that day.* Never had a boyfriend before him, no life experience, basically went from my father's lap to his with nothing in between. And I don't regret it, except for the part where I'm learning how to be on my own now for the first time in my life. And I'm making a lot of mistakes, I know. I'm trying, but...I don't think I know who I am apart from Kaine. I get the unsettling feeling I'm not such a good person on my own."

Aiden's standing a few feet from me looking away toward the doors, and when I stop talking I see his shoulders straighten like he's settling into his resolve. Resolve for what I don't know, but I figure it can't be good.

"Stop using him as an excuse."

"What?"

"You think you don't have an identity of your own but the truth is you do, you just don't like it. You're blaming him for who you are now but you've been split up for how long, almost a year? That's long enough to figure a few things out and make changes on the parts you don't like, Clarissa. When Sarah kicked me out I stayed stoned for a month and then I faced facts, accepted what I saw in the mirror and moved on. I *choose* to be what I am. I dunno how good it is, but at least I know I'm doing my best and whatever I do wrong is my own damn fault."

"Aiden, it's not that simple - "

I'm about to launch into all the reasons why my life as a slayer in the tutelage of an ancient demi-immortal with a fetish for sharp things doesn't quite fall into the self help fixer-upper category when a nauseating shift under my feet sends me staggering into the nearest wall. While I'm getting my bearings back I realize two things -

- the floor didn't just move, it *rippled*...

...and something is now standing behind me, its heavy breath rustling my hair right before a huge hand wraps itself completely around my neck.

Make that three things, because the lobby suddenly isn't the lobby anymore and I'm staring through a paneled glass wall into the Genealogy section, and Aiden is nowhere in sight.

"Hello slayer."

CHAPTER NINETEEN

The body behind me is gigantic, I can sense it towering over me with a height to rival Kaine. Male obviously, by the deep rumbling voice. Werewolf definitely, from the overpowering scent of cloves and coriander so strong it's assaulting my tastebuds. A Master undoubtedly, judging by the sheer power and strength in the hand that's lifting me off the floor with all the effort it takes to toss a stuffed animal off the bed.

I know I'm screwed.

I drive myself backwards into him and lodge my back to his chest so I can use both him and the wall in front of me for leverage, but he spins me around and sends me staggering across the hallway with a well placed boot against my ass.

Embarrassing. I regain my footing and get my first look at him, a loud gasp popping out of my mouth like a damn amateur despite my training and experience with his kind.

Even more embarrassing.

This one's more than a Master.   He's huge, a massive wall of humanoid flesh that I know will be twice this current size two seconds after he decides to shift into his true form.   He doesn't look old, but then neither does Kaine.

The leader I was meant to kill.

But I was supposed to cross over and take him out on his own side of the line, a page from the playbook that's obviously been torn out and set on fire now.   He's definitely standing on this side, and for a nervous few seconds I don't even know what I'm supposed to do about that.   So I keep my back to the wall, a standard level-one stance meant to prevent anyone from sneaking around and getting behind you, and take a quick inventory of what's in front of me.

He's ridiculously handsome in a battered war-torn sort of way.   Unrelentingly huge.   Visible scars on his face, his neck, his arms...his leather clothing covers everything else but I figure there's enough battlemarks on the rest of him to tell a long-ass story I don't have time to hear today.   He also has a copious amount of tattoos, tribal markings and runes that I'm sure mean something as profound and horrifying as the ones on Kaine's body.   His hair is long and shaggy and the color of a mountain wolf, and he's got an unkempt beard that touches his chest at the V of his battered black leather vest.   Werekind have always been the fashion inspiration for bikers since the dawn of the

Harley lifestyle, and this one looks like he invented the look himself.

And he's watching me with a grin that shakes me right down to my boots.

I've fought werewolves. They're not my specialty, but I've taken on my share over the years, mainly because Kaine never allowed me to pass anything off to him without at least giving it an honest effort before I bailed. It was his version of on the job training and though it came perilously close a time or two, it had never quite gotten me killed.

Until today. Kaine isn't here but his training is still with me, ingrained so deeply into my psyche that I couldn't forget it if I tried. If this wolf wants to fight me, I'm going to give him his fight without even thinking about it because that's how I've been taught. I'm going to lose like a bitch and probably pretty quick too, but the giant lycan is going to stand over my corpse after it's over and be damn well impressed at how well somebody trained this stupid human.

It's then that I notice his eyes are two different colors. A jagged scar, probably a very old one by the pale color of it, splits the left side of his face from brow to cheekbone. The fact that it also splits his left eye gives me a shudder that I can barely hide.

"What's your name?"

"What's yours?"

I don't know why I asked, really - I'm not likely to survive this encounter but if I do, I want to be able to tell Kaine who I met today.   A lycan Master stepping into our world is something to report to the higher-ups, though I suspect at this point in time Kaine is pretty much the highest higher-up still breathing.   Most of the other slayers, including his bosses, have buggered off one way or another, either died or gone into hiding or just outright retired since the Purge.

The Purge that was supposed to have permanently banished everyone of the non-human variety to the other side of the rift, with the exception of the occasional shifter or nightcrawler slipping through quietly to joyride on the bright side while thumbing their nose at the handful of gatekeepers left standing.   The same rift that is now apparently standing wide open in the middle of the Van Alta public library, letting guys like this stupidly huge werewolf step across in broad daylight like they own the place.

While I'm standing there catching my breath and watching him, those unsettling eyes drift down my body and he cocks his head to one side.   His rude stare chills me and an almost overwhelming urge to cover myself like I'm naked shudders through me.

"You had a baby recently?"

I shoot him a death glare as that stare glides across my breasts and settles on my stomach.   The last of the baby weight never did come off even though it's been four years - and high on the list of things I don't need is a giant barbarian-looking Otherworlder judging me for it. Kaine taught me to fight dirty and even though all I want right now is to lay this lycan's jugular open, I realize the pause in the action isn't an unwelcome thing to my overtaxed lungs. I'm not about to tell him about my kids though. *Never give them anything to use.*

He grins, and for one panicked second I hope to god he's not a thoughtstealer.

"Why'd they send you after me?"

"They didn't." I let my eyes move past him for a second, focusing on the white haired man sitting on the other side of the glass partition. The immortal. "I'm not here for you, though now that you've shown yourself on the wrong side of the line I'm going to have to add you to the list. But technically I'm here for him because he's the one I keep catching trespassing out here."

He looks behind him.

"My uncle Augustine? He likes to read the papers, what do you want with him?"

Recognition makes me blink hard. We have a very short list of holy abominations and this guy's on it, which would be something of an honor for me if he wasn't breaking all kinds of rules just by perusing the damn Sunday Times in the presence of humans. "He's *Augustine*?"

128

"Yeah."

"The last of the Sainteds."

"Yeah. So?"

"He's not supposed to be here, and neither are you."

"Maybe so, but I still don't get why they sent *you*." There's a sneering derision in his voice and under it I hear all the things he didn't put into words. *Female. Ridiculously small in the body and stupidly big in the mouth. Highly trained but not that strong. Carrying an ancient Slayer's mark but only half of the skills, if you're being generous.*

His tone is entirely correct. I've got the mark of Kaine, and I can see by the look on his face that he knows it. Recognition by scent, likely. He growls the name under his breath, all venom and hatred and a dangerous displeasure at having it in his mouth before he spits it out. I can sense the history here and I know it's got nothing to do with friendship and high esteem.

"Kaine's out of the game, I'm what you get now," I interject before my own annoyance causes an incident. Apparently I've forgotten about handing in my dramatic resignation last night and my own words hitting my ears make me furious - this is some kind of a new record for me, going back on my vow less than half a day after making it. "Unless you want Agent Earnest, he doesn't seem very eager to play though."

He sniffs the air, frowning as he tries to figure out who he's smelling in the lingering aura of every person that has set foot in the library over the last few days. It only takes him a few seconds to separate the one he's looking for from the rest. "Ah...Fitzpatrick." The scowl of distaste on his face is almost comical, but I don't get a chance to ask why the scent is making him look like he's going to throw up before he points to his left eye, the blue one, and then jabs his finger at me. "Kaine took my eye. Do you know how hard it is to park a car with no depth perception?"

"I imagine you stand out just a bit on public transport."

He laughs softly, completely out of sync with the overall menacing imagery he's exuding. It's disconcerting and I have to put some real effort into not taking a step back, though my back is still against the wall and there's no place for me to go. He reaches out one huge hand and points at my stomach, bringing us back to the original subject.

"So how old is your pup?"

"Not your concern."

"It might be." He snaps his teeth at me and I see fangs, big long ones. All my motherly instincts go on red alert but I know he's playing with me, so I keep my head cool and my hand on my hilt behind me. Werewolves love to talk shit but they're blessedly slow to back it up with action.

"You a fleshrender?"

He doesn't answer, but the hungry glint in his mismatched eyes tells me more than I want to know. Fleshrenders are at the very top of the list of illegals. Nasty monsters. Coming across and scaring the shit out of the humans is one thing, coming across and eating them is another kettle of nope entirely.

I'm going to have to put some honest effort into trying to kill this one.

And that makes me nervous, because he's twice my weight - easily - and has about two feet on me in height. His beef with Kaine is just one more odd stacked against me, but at this point in time he doesn't know I'm anything more than just another slayer acquainted with at least one Ancient. There's not a doubt in my head that if he knew I was married to the guy, I'd be dead already or dangled from a hook to lure his nemesis into the lair.

"You know your kind aren't allowed over here." My eyes fall to his neck and yep, sure enough, there's a restrainer branded into the skin below his left ear, proving that he's well known with the authorities and has been deemed too dangerous to take any risks with. The restrainer should be preventing him from crossing the line without a nasty shock to the cerebral cortex meant to shut his brain down entirely, but here he is, standing a good fifteen feet from the shimmering dimensional tear and staring at me like I'm dinner. I'd be confused if I didn't already know the answer to the question I should be asking.   He answers it anyway.

"It's coming down, baby.   The whole damn thing, all the way to the northern border.   There's about to be a whole new immigration problem and it's going to be coming through right here."   He steps back through the doorway into the Genealogy section and I think for a second that our encounter is over - but he stops next to Row H and turns back again to give me a wicked grin as his hand sparks and shivers and then disappears as he pushes it through the invisible wall that we both know is there.   Augustine laughs quietly from behind his newspaper and I know I'm screwed good and proper, the realization seeping in that I'm alone in the far side of a mostly empty building with a fleshrender and a soulstealer both within disemboweling distance.   One I can handle, maybe a bit sloppily, but I have good training behind me.   But two -

Two would be a challenge even for Kaine.

"What do you want?"

He smiles, and it's probably the scariest thing I've ever seen in my life.

"The world, babe.   The whole damn world."

CHAPTER TWENTY

Aiden doesn't answer his phone until the seventh ring, which is just about how long it takes for me to decide he died in that weird little isolated earthquake in the library and start trying to remember what the first stage of grief is. I can't recall if it's shock or denial, so I just skip them both and go straight to annoyed.

He answers on seven, his voice sleepy and caught halfway through a yawn that slaps my eardrum, and I realize time moved a bit weird while I was in Genealogy. He's obviously been home and asleep for a while.

"Did you survive?"

"Yeah, did you?"

"Yeah. Where did you go?"

"I dunno, we were in the lobby and then you weren't."

"You never left the lobby?"

"I don't think so. I stayed there for a while then looked around for you, went home about an hour later."

Huh. He looked for me. That was something - Kaine was known to walk off the scene of a battle and go home to eat before verifying that I was alive and well. I was going to have to find a way to keep this one.

"Okay listen, I need you to do some more research on the fault lines under the building - I think they're shifting and every time they do it probably widens the rift."

"Yeah, okay. Clarissa?"

"Yeah?"

"I want to talk to you, okay? Not about this stuff. Other stuff. Soon, alright?"

So many alarms go off in my head that my eye twitches. When a man wants to talk to you about something that isn't what's currently happening, your options are show up and hope for the best or pretend you don't know him and avoid that side of town for a while. But Aiden's got skills I need, so disavowing all knowledge of his existence is off the table. That plus he looked for me for an hour, which counts for something. "Okay sweetie, sure. The bar, tonight?"

"Yeah. Be there, okay?"

"I will."

I stare at the screen for what feels like hours, then open the dialer and call Kaine.

"Why am I here?"

"The library.   The rift is doing weird stuff, I think you should go have a look at it."

"Call your stoner bitch, I'm sure he'd do it for a blowjob."

I stare at him, struggling to keep my mouth shut and my temper dialed down.   The last thing I need this close to the apocalypse is my ex husband getting into a brawl in the Rite-Aid parking lot with every guy I've glanced at since the divorce.   But I need his help, and I won't be getting it unless I step very carefully around his cranky ass.

I'm back in the game whether I want to be or not.   And I really need him to be, too.

"There's a fleshrender in the library, he says he's Augustine's nephew."

The glass in Kaine's hand shatters, exploding all over him, the cranberry juice he just poured soaking his shirt so that he looks like he's been hit by a shotgun blast.   He's staring at me like I'm the one that shot him.

"The Sainted's blood?"

"If that's what being Augustine's nephew means, then yeah."

"Shit."

"Bad, huh?"

His face has gone dark and he takes a long time to answer, and I know he's struggling not to pick up anything that even remotely resembles a weapon and head straight for the library himself.   The nod he offers me is barely perceptible, but the crack in his voice exposes every bit of anger and fear and rage I know he's feeling as it dawns on him who exactly I just met.

"Did he have a - ?"   He points to his left eye.

"He's mad that he can't park his car."

"Shit."   His head falls to his hands for a second, and when he raises it he drags his fingers down his face hard enough to leave red streaks.   "What the hell is Fausto doing crossing over this early?   He's *tagged*.   He's a last resort."

"Sort of like you?"   The frantic look in his eyes is making me nervous - because if Kaine is anything but calm, the world is about to go up in flames.   There's no two ways about it.

"Listen to me Clary, listen very carefully.   If the Othersiders have decreed Fausto their leader, there aren't enough gravestones on the planet to mark all the dead we're going to be stepping over once they start flooding in here."

"We?"

"You'll be stepping over me, sweetheart.   Fausto and I have an awkward history between us."

"I figured that.   Is this why Fitzpatrick wants you to go into hiding?"

"He what?"

"He said they want you to go into hiding.   The general gist of it was that you're marked and they'd prefer not to lose you if at all possible."

"Fitz shouldn't care what I do."

"Why, did you get him killed in a past life?"   He doesn't answer but the sideways warning glance he shoots me is enough to tell me he's figured out who Not Bad Earnest is to him.   The Fitz that he used to know.   Kaine doesn't just randomly shorten people's names, if he's tagged you with a nickname you're someone he's either willing to die for or you've died for him, and since I know he's not a secondlifer himself...Fitz has met a demise at some point in their history.   For him or because of him, it's yet to be revealed.   And that's a story I'm dying to hear, because

137

Kaine's past is more violently colorful than a four year old puking the morning after Halloween. "You did, didn't you? You killed him or you sent him into a situation he didn't walk out of, and now he's got a job watching you and there's no way to tell if he's sincerely trying to keep you alive or he's doublecrossing you."

The look he levels at me is chilling and I know the unspoken answer is a resounding yes. So now I'm operating with a set of facts that involve my ex husband's tainted history with both a dimensional agent and a half blind werewolf, all sitting neatly on top of his newly revealed hatred of my somewhat partner Aiden - who is now, according to him, my stoner bitch. I know I'm going to have to keep those two apart because Aiden might make a decent lowfat caramel macchiato, but I have my doubts about his Krav Maga skills.

"Come to bed with me."

My head whips up and I stare at him in shock, though there's nothing in my history with Kaine that makes this something I haven't heard a million times before in a million less appropriate situations. Kaine is the king of making moves in the middle of whatever life or death situation we're currently drowning in; it's one of those last minute life affirming things that either reawakens your desire to stay alive or acknowledges the fact that it's never a bad idea to get laid one more time before you die.

And I'm the queen of doing what he says.   It's not a request and his tone makes that abundantly clear.   It's also an abrupt change of subject and that knocks me off balance and snaps my brain back into workplace mode.

"Excuse me?   We're not married anymore if you'll recall, we dissolved that vicious little union six months ago and you signed the papers - "

His heavily frustrated sigh overlaps my complaint and he changes his tone, but leaves the words the same.   The question mark tacked onto the end doesn't do much to sway me though so he says it again, softer this time, with an almost gentleness in his eyes that might work if I wasn't immune to it.   Goddamn that look.   It was a hard fought battle to develop thick enough skin to bounce it off me without the visceral kneejerk response it used to pull out of me, but I got there and so help me I'm not going back for anything.

"No."

"Come on Clary...I'm not asking you to marry me again."

"And thank god for that."

He moves over to me so quickly and smoothly that I don't even realize he's shifted spots until he's right in front of me, one hand taking mine to squeeze my fingers while the other comes up to caress my cheek with the back of his knuckles.   I flinch without thinking and he freezes, his eyes locked to my face, a grimace of absolute pain turning his handsome features into something almost difficult to look at. But this time it's not because I've slipped a blade into his back.

It's something else entirely, and far more painful for both of us.

He remembers, and he knows I do too.

"I'm sorry Clary," he whispers, removing his hand from my face. "That was something I never thought I would do to you."

I don't want him to say it so I nod my head and steel up, keeping my expression carefully blank so neither of us has to go there. But he's already around that corner, and when his eyes go to my cheekbone I see it there in the icy blue of his stare.

He remembers that night as clearly as I do. And though it hurts him in an entirely different way than it hurts me, the pain is still real and raw and neither of us is ever going to get over it. His guilt is as vicious as my recollection of the bruise I wore for a month, the same exact size and shape as the knuckles of his left hand, right where he just touched me. And then I hear it in the slight tremor that haunts the dark depth of his voice, and all I can do is close my eyes and swallow hard.

"Don't, Kaine."

"I have to Clary. I did some terrible things to you."

"Yeah well - I did my share back to you. We can call it even and get back to work now."

He's shaking his head, his hand on the side of my neck now holding me. "I hurt you sweetheart. You trusted me and I betrayed that."

"Don't. I mean it...*don't*."

His mouth comes to mine and I feel his lip tremble, and that's it for me. Kaine is my weakness, he always has been and apparently he always will be. I've seen this man show heavy emotion a grand total of three times in the thirty years I've been with him and a fourth is the absolute last thing I want to witness, so I bring my hands up and slam them hard against his chest to push him away from me.

He's having none of that. In less than the space of a heartbeat I'm up against the counter next to the stove and that tentative touch of his lips against mine has turned into something I'm not going to be able to get out of unless I kill him now. But Kaine isn't easy to kill - I know because I've tried - and just before my brain resets to zero it flashes an image of Aiden sitting in the bar, turning his glass slowly while he waits just five more minutes for me.

(HAPTER TWENTY ONE

I know I'm damned, and if I'm not I sure as hell should be.

I'm a terrible person.   I'm laying in bed next to my ex - whom I've sworn off of at least a dozen times in the space of the last few weeks - and my part time lover and research analyst is probably at home right now with a bottle of something cheap and potent, wondering why he ever said hi to me at that damn group meeting and making yet another oath to never trust me again.   But it's three in the morning and Kaine, for all his surly growling and gruff unpleasant disposition, is stroking a long finger up and down my hip just lightly enough to send a shiver through my entire body and make me forget how rotten I feel about all of it.

Damn him.

"So what did you do to Fitz, I gotta know."

Kaine rolls over onto his back and something vaguely reminiscent of a chuckle rumbles in his throat.   I've never heard him chuckle before.   I've barely ever even seen the man smile, but he's grinning right now and it's every bit as oddly arousing as it is unnerving. "I may have beheaded him in 1612. And possibly again in 1726."

Oh.

"Well that's...not entirely unexpected. I've known him for all of about three months and I'd like nothing better than to behead him a couple of times." I look over at him and wonder what's going through his head right now. He's staring at the ceiling and there's the closest thing Kaine can muster to a mischievous grin tugging at his mouth. "I'm gonna see him on Friday, is there anything else I should know before I talk to him again?"

"1863. Allegedly."

Dear god. "So were the 1900's a time-out century? Dude went into hiding, got himself an iron turtleneck?"

"There might have been an incident in '71 but again...*alleged*."

Geezus. No wonder the guy watches me with such calculating menace in those cold blue eyes of his, every time he looks at me he probably gets a sore throat. "Well, it sounds like he's due again and to be honest I wouldn't call the cops if I saw it happen. Guy's a bit of a dick."

"Does he still have bad eyesight?"

"Glasses like Coke bottle bottoms."

He huffs out a vicious little laugh and I'm set to start asking questions when the mood goes all kinds of not-conducive. Kaine turns onto his side again and slides a hand down between my legs, a signal that I know means story time is over.   But I can't help but wonder which part of this scenario has him turned on more - the memories of vanquishing Fitz at least once a century for the last few hundred years, or the fact that there's a warm willing female spreading her legs to his invading fingers.

I don't guess it matters, really...the end result is going to be the same either way.

I pick up my phone from the bedside table while Kaine is resettling the pillows and send Aiden a text to meet me at the Genealogy section as soon as the library opens in the morning.   He doesn't reply, but I don't really expect him to.

(HAPTER TWENTY TWo

I'm late to the library, not surprisingly.   The morning sun is appallingly cheerful and refuses to allow me my sullen emotional rainclouds without an argument that I know I'm going to lose.   I know Aiden is going to be standing outside the Genealogy section when I finally get there, patience oozing out of that laid back personality of his even though he has every right to be pissed with me for standing him up.   I also know I'm going to try to apologize to him, and that he's going to shrug in that *Ehh no worries, life's like that* kind of way he has, and we're going to step awkwardly around each other until my conscience sends me to the ladies room under the guise of an IBS flareup just to get away from him.   Because memories of the night I just spent making love in every conceivable way with my ex husband are going to reach up and slap me every time I look at Aiden's sweet face, and he's going to know why I didn't show up last night.

Guilt shouldn't really be coming into play here and I know it - Aiden and I don't have any sort of agreement between us outside of sorting the library situation and a bit of stress-reducing extracurriculars from time to time - but it's a tough thing to hold off when you're working in close proximity with the guy you probably *should* have slept with.

He looks up at me as the corridor doors swing shut behind me and there it is, that knowing look, the one that starts at my eyes and falls briefly to my crotch and then quickly elsewhere, anywhere but at me. He knows I've been with Kaine as surely as if he can smell him on me. I take a quick inventory sniff of myself to make sure he can't and then push quickly past the incidentals.

"You know what you're here for, right?"

"Another round of emotional abuse? Oh no wait, that's probably coming later. Right now I'm supposed to look into the maw of Hades and tell you what it ate for breakfast, right?"

"Aiden - "

He looks away, and I notice his eyes are sort of puffy and red. "Naw, leave it. I'm not sure my self pity hangover can compete with the ricochet echo of your self loathing and questionable choices in this small of a space. Somebody might get hurt."

The look in his eyes tells me someone already has. But we're not here in the hallway outside the Genealogy section for a seminar on soul searching and self actualizing realization...we're here to scope a potentially escalating situation for signs that things are about to go wretchedly sideways, and de-escalate them if we can.

I don't hold out much hope for that last bit, to be honest. But I'm officially out of my very brief retirement, and I've got a sidekick who can see into the rift and probably has a pocket full of something potent for afterwards.

I'd ask what could possibly go wrong if I didn't already know the answer is *literally everything*.

We're just about two steps inside the Genealogy section when that whole *wretchedly sideways* scenario grabs us around the throat.   Or me, anyway.   I know the fist compressing my trachea belongs to the same ridiculously muscled monster I met the other night - there's an overwhelming burst of cloves and coriander and testosterone charged male virility that I instantly recognize - and while I'm calculating how far my feet are from the floor I hear Aiden's surprised yelp from somewhere behind me.

The thought of him being handled the way I'm being handled makes me angry, and just about the time *Well that's new* is forming in my head, all that reactionary conditioning Kaine trained into me takes over.

The next thing to hit my conscious awareness is the fact that my feet are on the floor again and a big freaking Othersider is glaring at me like I'm a stray cat that just walked across his yard, and he's pulling my blade out of his forearm where it's lodged between the ulna and radius. But Aiden is okay, if not resoundingly horrified by what he just saw me do. He's standing against the wall staring at me.

"Holy *shit* Clarissa."

There are moments in our day to day lives when clarity hits and things go so shockingly bright in our heads that all we can do is think *This is it, this is one of those moments of truth that the rest of my life hinges on.* It's what we do with those moments that dictate whether or not we walk away unscathed or tumble ass-end over skullbone into disaster.

This is one of those moments, and it's already clear I won't be copping the unscathed option. What was the big guy's name? Kaine had said it...

Fausto.

Fausto is slowly turning his head from Aiden back to me with that scar-cracked eyebrow hitched in sudden comprehension and it's obvious I'm not the only one having a clarity moment. Something has just been

148

confirmed for him, and I know what it is before he even opens his mouth and speaks it into existence.

"So you're the Carmichael woman.   Well well."

Yep, I'm well and truly screwed.

"I'm guessing your next words are going to be something blatantly and obnoxiously sexist, probably along the lines of 'So you're Kaine's female', like I'm verified solely by the fact that we share a last name.   Am I right?   And by the way, your uncle already knew.   You guys should communicate better."

The sneer that breaks his face is chilling.

"Bring the Macedonian to me."

Not what I was expecting.   Aiden whispers "Macedonian?" and the big werewolf's eyes shift from me to him again.

"They call Kaine the Macedonian because that's where he's from," I explain, stalling for a little time while my head and senses wrap themselves around the circumstances at hand.   "Back when...you know...it was an empire."   I can feel the situation slowly settling into a less aggressive sort of lull as Fausto slowly wraps his quickly healing injury with the bottom of his shirt - and there's nothing bad about that. Fewer people get killed during less aggressive lulls.

The sigh that drifts from Aiden's mouth might as well have come from his heart, it's such a resigned and hopeless sound. "Right. I'm guessing everyone in here has seen a minimum of two world wars and at least one martyred saint."

"That would be my uncle," Fausto offers, gesturing toward the sofa where the immortal sits reading yesterday's newspaper like there wasn't just blood spilled fifteen feet away. "Augustine's the only saint in this room, martyred or otherwise, and he's definitely the oldest one here...but he won't be once you bring me Kaine."

"Augustine?" There's an excited recognition in Aiden's voice and I know he's starting to accept the facts I've been conditioning into him - that this world is full of weird shit and the craziest option you can come up with to explain any given situation is just as likely as not to be the correct one - and the irrepressible curiosity of his nerdy side is about to override the terror any normal human would be feeling right about now. "*That* Augustine? The guy who confessed for three days about all the shit he did when he was a teenager?"

The immortal's head whips up and he snarls at Aiden. "It's called a conscience, boy."

"It's called overkill guilt and you were obviously stalling for time - what was really going on that you were distracting everyone from?"

"Aiden, now's not the time."

"Why not? Do you realize this guy's writings were the major influence for Western philosophy and Christianity?"

"All the more reason for me to send him back across the line."

Augustine growls, but I'm past feeling threatened by anyone present. There's about to be a verbal throwdown in Genealogy, and as much as I'd love to spend the next three days hearing what the deposed saint has to say for himself, we don't have time for this. "Okay lets pull back real hard on the reins here before this whole thing veers off into a philosophical discussion on the unnecessary virtue of outing oneself and sort why this big one here wants Kaine and why he thinks I can supply him, because FYI, I can't."

Fausto is staring at the finger I'm pointing at him, and it's taking all the strength of will I've got not to yank my hand back out of range when he snarls, "You can and you will, otherwise I make pretty boy here my bitch."

Aiden doesn't even miss a beat, the shock of everything worn off and a bold resignation taking its place. "Sorry, I'm already *her* bitch."

Those disturbingly mismatched eyes come back to me and it's all I can do not to shudder. Something about that pale blue iris creeps me out; the fact that Kaine gave it to him makes it that much worse. Werewolves are notoriously bad about making friends, relatives, distant acquaintances, and future offspring pay for wrongs committed against them - and from this one's attitude toward me, I can tell he wouldn't think twice about ripping my uterus out for dinner as a warning shot across Kaine's bow.   Since I'm ovulating, I'd probably not only let him but suggest it as an option.

"Kaine is his own boss these days, I rarely see him."   *Except when I'm sleeping with him.   Or training with him.   Or arguing with him.   Or sleeping with him again.   Geezus Clarissa, I hope this guy can't smell lies.*   I send a mental message to Aiden, though I doubt he can hear me and I wouldn't blame him if he blew it off anyway.   *Don't you say a word.*

"Bullshit," Fausto growls.   "You and him spawned progeny together, Kaine would be the last to walk away from his litter."

Aiden's getting more and more confused as the conversation progresses, I can feel the befuddlement just billowing off him in waves.   "Litter?"

"This one's a lycan, they reproduce the same way dogs do."

"Not anymore," Fausto interrupts with a fierce scowl that makes it clear this is a touchy subject for him.   "The Other Side is no longer...conducive...to progenitive activity."

"Good.   You should have never been given the ability to reproduce to begin with."

I know as soon as the words have left my mouth that I should have thought that one through a little better.

"Why? Because we're abominations? You think you have the right to get righteously indignant because the Maker was kind to us for a little while?" The look of pure disgust that pulls his face into an unnerving likeliness of a feral wolf almost makes me reach for my backup, the jagged tanto tucked into the closure strap of my bra; Aiden moves to my side, but he doesn't step back behind me like I expect him to.

He steps in *front* of me.

There are no words for a long, high stress few moments while he and Fausto stare each other down, and in the fourth or fifth heartbeat of that frozen bit of time I realize something horrible.

I'm going to get Aiden killed.

"I'll give your message to Kaine, but whether or not he shows up is his choice." I'm tugging at the back belt loop of Aiden's jeans, but he's not letting me move him and Fausto's eyes are burning straight through his head. "Something tells me he isn't going to want to waste his time."

"You do that, female. And you should put your bitch on a chain before I breed him." He snaps his teeth at Aiden, then his ferocious glare melts into a laugh. "Now you best get out of here before the fun starts."

As soon as we step out into the shaded sun of a brewing early storm I punch Aiden in the shoulder so hard that he careens into the rose bushes.

"*Never* do that again."

"What did I do?"

"You seem to have a stray and completely misguided sense of chivalry with just a dollop of *gonna get my ass straight up murdered,* Aiden.   Don't you *ever* get between me and an Othersider again or I'll disembowel you myself."

"Sorry, I wasn't thinking."

"Do you really think you'd last two seconds if that beast in there went ballistic?   He's an *Ancient,* Aiden.   He's got skills you haven't even read about in sci-fi compendiums because there aren't words for them in any of the common languages yet.   He can kill you in about fourteen different ways before you even realize he's blinked.   *And he would.*"   I stomp over and slap him again, hard, on the side of the neck over the jugular where it stings worst.

"Ouch, damn.   I'm sorry."

He's cowering just a little, which strikes me as funny in light of the fact that he just stood face to face with a werewolf not five minutes ago.   I don't know if he assumes the whole incident was a hallucination from too much weed or if he really grasps the truth of it - that he, a mortal human, just met a creature that's been written about and referred to in horror stories since the beginning of time.   And the idiot got in the monster's face.   For some reason that makes me feel a little bit funny in the frilly unmentionables, but I'm too angry at the implications of taking on a sidekick who potentially doesn't believe what he's seeing.

I need Aiden to believe.

But first I need him to learn how to fight, because he's got a little girl who looks just like him and I'll be damned if I'll take another father away from his children.

CHAPTER TWENTY THREE

Maybe a month has gone by, two possibly, since my second encounter with the werewolf and I'm getting anxious waiting for something to happen. Life has been moving the way it should, at normal speed or maybe a tiny bit slower, and for a brief little while I entertain the fantasy that maybe, just *maybe*, this is how things are meant to be. Just a regular life with regular people, doing regular things.

Not likely, not for me...but it's something I wouldn't mind trying. The back and forth status of my retirement is starting to give me whiplash though, and I'm slightly disappointed that maybe it's on again.

Kaine is staying on his side of the fence, metaphorically speaking. He takes the boys every third day, picks them up at school when I can't or don't want to, eats dinner with us on weekends when it suits him. He treats me different now, with less animosity and more indifference. It's as if he's finally let go of us and has begun the process of pulling away, though he appears to have skipped the first few stages of retraction and gone straight to *ehh whatever.*   The fact that he should probably be in hiding instead of showing up at my house every few days in broad daylight to take the kids out for laser tag concerns me for about a minute and a half, and then I remember this is Kaine we're talking about.   Hiding isn't his thing.   His thing runs more along the lines of strutting down the middle of main street at high noon with guns blazing, and that's something that's always worked for him.

I never delivered Fausto's message, and the Macedonian hasn't been handed over to him, and for all I know everything's been called off and everyone's gone home - though the bigger part of my common sense doubts it and the sneaking suspicion hanging around the back of my skull keeps whispering that this is the still before the storm.

It's a convincing stillness, though.

Fitz asks me every week at group if the old slayer's taking his advice to heart, and every week I roll my eyes and pour myself another cup of coffee and tell him to call Kaine and ask him himself, because the man sure as hell doesn't listen to me anymore - not that he ever really did.   I even give Fitz his phone number, but the dark look in the Agent's eyes makes it abundantly clear he has no intention of getting in any kind of contact with his blade-happy former acquaintance.   The nervous neck-rub thing he does gives me a little bit of a giggle, though.   Every damn time.   He drops the napkin with Kaine's number in the trashcan by the door on his way out.

The library remains quiet, no unnerving echoes from Genealogy, no early evening strolls down the corridors by beings that shouldn't be walking this side in the daylight. Marta removes the Section Closed sign from the long hallway at the east end of the building and Aiden and I stare at it, brightly lit and holding tightly to its secrets, each time group lets out for coffee. We're not sure what to do now, so we just keep showing up, listening with fake smiles of encouragement to the stories that are now somehow worse than our own. Neither of us has any interest in Miss Hailey Wilcox's sunshiny self help rhetoric. We just want to stay close to the rift in the hope that eventually something will happen.

After a while that hope starts to fade.

I toy with the idea of getting a job of some kind just to fill my spare hours and keep my head busy and my trigger finger occupied, though I don't have a clue what sort of work I would be cut out for - I've never had a job in my life, Kaine has always had money from some undisclosed source that I've never asked about. He's hinted a time or two that some ill-advised and probably highly illegal venture in the mid sixteenth century ended in his favor to a point where he and anyone he cares to care for will be conceivably set for this life and fifteen more beyond it, and I've never pushed for details. Now that we're no longer together, cash appears on the kitchen countertop under the sugar canister on a regular basis. I don't ask about that either. I just drink a lot, avoid the library on any day that isn't a group meeting, agonize over my apparent lack of a conscience where bouncing back and forth between Aiden and Kaine is concerned, and sink a little lower into the dark grave of my nonexistent self esteem while life moves on around me.

It ain't healthy, but it'll do until something better comes along.

Aiden is still mad at me, and I can't say I blame him for his righteous indignation.   If anything in the history of relationships has been valid and justified, it's his hurt feelings.   We sit through group in silence, not speaking unless we're spoken to, neither of us volunteering anything other than an occasional nod of sympathy or support for the others in attendance.   A couple of the women eye us suspiciously, as if they've figured out there's something uncomfortable between us and they're dying for details. The library's been so quiet now, so unwilling to provide us with anything to keep us entertained, and to be honest I think we only keep going for the free coffee and cookies.

Maybe it's habit.   Maybe it's the clinging hope that one night we'll hear something from outside those glass panels that we shouldn't be hearing.   But in between meetings Aiden researches the library's history and I try to teach him basic combat maneuvers on the hopes of keeping him alive until this thing is over, knowing that sooner or later that rift is going to start spewing out trouble again, both of us carrying the unsettling knowledge that something is watching from the Genealogy section...something that isn't going to stay in there forever.   We can slip out of the building and rush home right after meetings as much as we want, but nothing is going to slow down what's coming once it finally decides to come.

We plan to be ready for it, but the silence from that long hallway is starting to sound a lot like nothing.

Eventually the lack of activity gets to Kaine, and things go off the rails.   Not just your typical train wreck - when Kaine loses it, there are explosions and fire raining from the sky and entire cities leveled into piles of smoking rubble.   I've seen it, and it's never pretty.   Impressive, absolutely.   But not pretty.   Which is why the form this particular bit of drama takes upon itself comes as such a shock to me, and why I'd do just about anything to erase it.

"Why are you in my house?"

I don't hear him come in - I never do, it's just one of those Kaine things that you accept and get used to - but he's got no reason to be in my house in the middle of the night smelling like good Scotch and crawling into my bed like the pillow on the left side is still his. I push back against the solid body behind me as hard as I can, but it doesn't move and I know before it even speaks that it's him. "You don't live here anymore you know."

"My name is still on the mailbox." His voice is deep and rumbly and confirms that there's been a bottle of something strong and wicked involved in this little bout of temporary insanity. He absolutely shouldn't be here, up in my personal space, all kinds of naked and putting his big warm hands on me while I'm half asleep.

"I'll fix that tomorrow."

"Until then it gives me the right to come in when I want."

"The restraining order says otherwise."

He laughs, and it's that slow, deep, unhurried laugh that has never in thirty something years failed to send a gush of warmth through me. Straight south. He snuggles up to my back and lays his arm over my waist from behind. "There isn't one."

"Only until I'm awake enough to make a phone call."

He ignores me while his hand slides down my hip. "The outside of your leg is always cold. Your body allocates heat so strangely."

"Yeah well. I'm part werewolf, didn't you know?"

His hand freezes and I feel his breathing stop. I don't know if he's plotting his next move or if he's deciding how he wants to kill me, because this is something we don't joke about. I've been near Fausto twice without Kaine present and I know he's running the math through his head right this moment. Have I been compromised?

Compromised. The polite word for dead man walking. If I've been bitten I'm a goner, and it'll be at Kaine's hands because the last thing we need is a converted Othersider running around on this side with the kind of knowledge I've got.

After a long silence during which neither of us move, his switch suddenly flips back.

"Lets make love Clary. I want you."

Here we go. Weeks of silence, of terse occasional coexistence and begrudging cooperation and sparring sessions handled so professionally you'd think he was a hired personal trainer, all boiling down to this.   *This* being the simple fact that Kaine is never going to be out of my system, and I'm never going to be out of his.

"I think that's always been part of the problem Kaine," I whisper, the words not wanting to rise any louder than the narrow space between my mouth and his ears calls for. "You've always wanted me.   You've never *needed* me. You were lonely, you wanted a partner, you recruited me to keep you company.   That's what I was to you."

"That's not entirely true and you know it."

Yeah.   My so-called skills were the bigger part of it, a.k.a. my total absence of fear and astounding adeptness at the suspension of disbelief.   The first time he showed me a Faeghoul I wasn't scared of it, I wanted to pat its head to see if the shimmer felt like fish scales or those sparkly discs you sew onto prom gowns.   And that turned him on so damn much, he had to keep me.

"Come on Clary," he purrs against the back of my head, pushing his hips against me in an evil rhythm that makes his voice that much harder to ignore.   "Sex, you, me…I know you remember how…all you have to do is spread your legs, we both know you're not out of practice."

Something explodes in the general region of my righteous indignation and I shove my elbow into the middle of his chest so hard he grunts.

"Get out!!"

"Oh for fucks sake - "

"Get out of my bed and out of my house, *now*."

"It's the middle of the night, Clary."

"That's what happens when you drive somewhere at three a.m. Kaine.   You got yourself here, get yourself gone."

There's an infuriating lack of obedience coming from his side of the bed so I give him a hard kick in the shin with the back of my heel; all it does is send a shooting pain through my foot and when his hands come up to my shoulders I know - I *know* - this is all about to go so very very wrong. Because the pathetic truth of it is that just feeling him push up against me has started the juices flowing, and if he presses the matter for a few more seconds I'm going to be a goner.   I'm going to have sex with him and it's going to be the usual insane mix of angry passion and nauseating intimacy, and in the morning I'm going to hate myself a whole lot more than I did when I went to bed.   Because Kaine is my downfall.   He's my kryptonite.   He's the oaken stake through my vampire heart, if I was a vampire.   And the worst part of it is he knows it.

And just like that, the lit fuse on the explosive rage I felt no more than thirty seconds ago goes out.

"Look, just - go sleep on the sofa."   The sudden softness in my voice makes me want to punch myself in the face but I can't stop, not until he's gone and takes this unwelcome and ill-advised round of feelings with him.   "Not in here.

Get out of this room, you can see the boys in the morning on your way out but *do* not wake me up."

"Clary - "

"*No.*"

The rustle of the bedsheets followed by the soft click of the door a few seconds later are both so heavy in their finality that I don't even bother getting up to lock him out.   He won't be coming back tonight.

Sleep stays mockingly out of my reach after he leaves, which irritates the piss out of me because I'd been sleeping so soundly before he crawled into bed with me.   I can't get that face out of my head, that sweet face with those big soulful eyes and that adorable crooked grin.

Not Kaine's face.

Aiden's.

Kaine's crude remark about me not being lacking in practice has dragged back a memory of the last time Aiden and I were together, the night he looked up at me while I rode him and told me he didn't understand why he couldn't walk away.   He knew he should.   I knew he should.   And it didn't even have much to do with the sex, even though that was pretty damn good as a standalone excuse whether either of us wanted to be shallow enough to acknowledge it or not.

Which must be why, after a groan of frustration, I swing my legs over the side of the bed and shove my feet into my fuzzy slippers.

And why seventeen minutes later I'm smiling sheepishly at Aiden as he stands sleepily blinking at me, before stepping aside so I can enter his apartment.

CHAPTER TWENTY FOUR

"I'm sorry Aiden, I just - " He's staring at me with mild concern, most likely because it's nearly four in the morning and I'm at his place in my pajamas. I stare down at my fuzzy slippers, fidgeting. "Kaine showed up at my place and he wouldn't leave."

The mild concern turns to open worry and he reaches for me. *Oh god, not a good idea.*

"Shit Clarissa, are you okay?"

I stare stupidly at him because I don't know what to say - am I okay? I've just kicked my ex, the former love of my life, out of my bed and then drove across town while the rest of the city slept like sane people to knock on the door of a guy I keep kicking in the emotional nutsack. I honestly don't know if I'm okay or not. I feel...uncomfortably numb.

A little bit sad, maybe.

And definitely a healthy dose of something else.

Possibly as a result of all of those factors clashing and crashing into one another in whatever part of me handles emotional response versus rational decision making, it somehow seems like a good idea - at the time anyway - to simply hurl myself at him in lieu of an answer. Our mouths crash together and his arms go around my back and quicker than my brain can catch up we're kissing, hard and fierce and more damn serious than either of us feels comfortable with. But neither of us is pulling back or slowing down, and the unbearable intimacy of our bodies rubbing against each other overrides every warning signal our brains are frantically sending out.

His hand slides up to my breast and I've just shivered from the tickle of his thumb teasing across my nipple when he asks, breathless in my ear, "Is this a booty call?"

It shocks me; I don't know what to say again, so once again I don't say anything, and in the next moment he *realizes* I'm not saying anything and pulls his head up to look at me.

"Is it?"

"I...I don't..."

There's a disappointed finality in the sigh that whispers from his lips as he steps back from me and shoves his hands into his hair, giving it a frustrated tug. "If you're confused, you shouldn't be here."

He's right. God, he's so right. "I...I'm sorry Aiden. Kaine just showed up and he wanted to have sex but I said no and...well he wouldn't leave, and he said something about you and me and I just..." All the pathetic coming out of my mouth is annoying me so much I can't even imagine what it's doing to him, but I'm not about to look at him to see. Blurting is best sometimes, and I can blurt with the best of them. "I couldn't stop thinking about you after that."

There's more melancholia than anger in his voice when he drops his gaze to the floor and whispers, *"Please don't use me."*

"Aiden...no..."

"I know you're used to badasses, but my heart can't take it."

He's not looking at me, and I wonder if he ever really will again. Because I've stretched Aiden's trust just about as far as I figure it's capable of going, and the hurt in those big blue eyes when they find mine again is so deep and achingly permanent that I feel sick to my stomach. I've wounded him, I've probably humiliated him, I've definitely used him, he's not mistaken about that...I don't know when I became who I am at this moment in time, but somewhere along the way I forgot that my drama with Kaine is just that - my drama with Kaine. Aiden is innocent. But somehow in the scuffle some of it has splashed on him.

"I'm sorry sweetie...I just...really...didn't want him.   And then I realized I wanted *you* - "

It's the truth, every word, and it surprises me more than him. Vulnerable is something I've never been and this feels so very very naked and exposed and painfully full of cringe, but stopping now that I've started isn't an option.   What exactly am I trying to say though?

I care about him?   There's no question about that, Aiden has become a good friend - supportive, trusting, willing to suspend disbelief pretty much every time I open my mouth and start talking.   He's walked beside me into some shaky situations and proven his mettle without being asked to. He's forgiven a lot more than he should and overlooked so many missteps on my part that it almost seems he has an automatic reset switch when it comes to letting me off the hook.

A good man, no doubt.

Is it more than that?

Do I *love* the guy?

Can't go there, not while Kaine is alive.   I like Aiden, a lot. There are feelings in there that could get messy if I let them, yes.   Can I acknowledge them?

Hell no.   It's becoming obvious that I'm never going to be over Kaine, I'm never going to move on.   But I'm here in Aiden's apartment and Kaine is asleep on my sofa across town, and there's only one of them I'm willing to be with tonight.   That has to mean something.

But for the life of me I can't put a name to it.

Even if I did, none of it is going to be fair to Aiden.

"You're just a really bright spot in a lot of darkness, and I think about you a lot."

He nods, a slow reluctant acceptance, but it's not in agreement.   At least not with my words.

He's agreeing with his own, before he says them.

"You should go home."

It's my turn to nod now.   There seems to be a lot of it going around and it just feels like the right thing to do now that we've started the trend.   At least it gives me a way to squirm out from under the embarrassing weight of what I just said.   "Yeah, I should.   I should just...go."

I'm looking around like I've forgotten something and when it comes to me I feel stupid, because it's the reason I'm here in the first place - and somewhere in all the awkward emotional avoidance it's completely slipped my head.   "No wait, I don't want to go home.   Kaine will be there till morning and I don't want to see him.   Can I just - "   I frantically peer around the room, my eyes falling to the sofa against the windows.   "I'll sleep on the couch.   Yeah, the couch will be good."

Me and Kaine, sacking out on sofas in other peoples' houses tonight. Ain't we a pair. But Aiden is Aiden, and he hasn't got an unchivalrous bone in his long lean body.

"No, you take the bed, I'll sleep on the couch."

He moves toward the hallway and I know he's going to the closet for blankets and a spare pillow, and before he can pass me I reach out to grab his arm - but I stop before I touch him, because I know by the way he isn't looking at me that my touch isn't something he wants right now. Or maybe he wants it, but he's beyond hoping I won't stomp on his feelings again the second I remember Kaine exists.

I really need some counseling.

"It's your bed. We can share, I'll keep my hands to myself. Promise."

I don't know if he believes me, but after a long pause during which I'm sure he's weighing all the possible ways this can go disastrous on him, he puts the final nod on our night and holds his hand out. But he's not holding it out to me. He's motioning toward the bedroom, giving me permission to go get in his bed.

I don't deserve Aiden Magnussen. I really truly don't.

CHAPTER TWENTY FIVE

"Your wife is an attorney?"

"Ex wife.   Yeah."

"Wow."   It's morning and I'm sitting at Aiden's kitchen bar, staring at him over a glass of orange juice that he convinced me would be better for me than coffee, not even trying to hide my shock at this little personal revelation.   Aiden, laid back stoner hippie boy deluxe, was married to a lawyer?   "Did she do your divorce?"

"No, an associate of hers did."

"Oh, yikes.   I guess you got laundered on the heavy duty cycle, huh."

"Pretty much, yeah."

"Wow."   I've said that twice, I know - but it's all that's coming to me, and Aiden has a slightly bored if not entirely un-bemused look on his face that says he's just as surprised by it as I am.   "What's an easygoing longhaired guy like you doing marrying a lawyer?"

"We shared a dorm in college."

Before my mouth can pop out the *Oh my god they were roommates* meme that my brain instantly latches onto, something else overrides the whole thing and my mouth, as usual, goes with the second one simply because it's the most shocking. "You went to college?"

The look he shoots me is more mildly hurt annoyance than put-out anger. "Is that so wildly unexpected?"

Yes, actually. I don't say it though, because he's making breakfast and I want what's in that pan more than I want to live. "What was your major?"

"Archaeology."

"Wow." I seem to be saying that a lot, but honestly the idea of Aiden in college and marrying an attorney is...sort of mindblowing. The archaeology thing just cherries it. "Did you finish?"

"Naw. My grades weren't good enough for them to keep throwing grant money at me. After a while I did us all a favor and dropped out."

"Well, you did better than me - I never even got to the point of applying for grants. Kaine recruited me straight out of high school."

He looks at me funny. "Is that how you see your marriage? A recruitment?"

There it is, the truth I wasn't searching for, spoken by a man with long hair and an *Indiana Jones Was A Graverobber, Fight Me* tee shirt, standing at a stove stirring scrambled eggs.   It's a jarring bit of realization.

Kaine recruited me.   He waited until I was old enough for two things: to face danger as a legal adult able to consent to the risk, and to marry as a legal adult able to consent to the union.   I'd often wondered if he'd married me so he would be able to drag me around the world hunting monsters without having to evade the cops for kidnapping and endangerment of a minor.   I was eighteen.   I was legal.   But just by a matter of days.

I knew I had skills he needed.   I knew he was lonely.   I knew he was tired of creeping through history under the radar without anything to classify him as something other than a rumor that might or might not have actually existed outside of legend.

Do ya love me, Kaine?

Love's a dangerous thing, Clary.   But yeah.   Now shut up and prime that crossbow again till you get it right.

Love was like that sometimes.   Wasn't it?   How the hell would I know…Kaine was my first, my last, my only.   I had nothing to compare him to, and so I took his word for it when he said this life was what I was meant for.   Life with him, hunting monsters that he told me deserved to die. Was he right about that?   Was he right about any of it?

For all I knew my ideas of passion and romance and literally everything else were every bit as skewered as the life I'd been told was normal.   Righteous even.

I'd never given the weirdness of it all a second thought.

Until now, sitting at the bar in Aiden's kitchen, feeling a little bit sad that the gentle mundane nature of watching this mild mannered man make me breakfast is tugging so hard at my heart.   That the night I just spent in his bed being held by him as I listened to him breathe is making me long for something boring and safe and tender and decidedly not what I'm used to.

Real romance, the kind that's just warm and quiet and seeps into your soul.

I'm not even really sure what I'm looking at, but something in me wants it.

Romance for me and Kaine had always involved highly modified medieval weaponry and chasing nightmares through back alleys in the dead of night.   More often than not - until our later years, when the kids started being born - our most intimate moments were spent sleeping rough on the hunt.   The sex was something that grounded us, brought us back to the common world, reminded us that we were human.   It was how we kept from losing ourselves - and each other - to the job.

The difference between that and the intimacy of sleeping next to Aiden is staggering.   Aiden is calm, warm, nurturing.

He holds me like I'm a delicate thing, even though I suspect he knows I'm not.   And he touches me as if I'm doing him an undeserved favor by just allowing him to be close.

He's the slow warmth of a campfire just beginning to kindle up.

Kaine is the blazing heat of a roaring bonfire gone out of control.

And me?   I'm the drunken moth flapping around with my wings on fire, too stupid to admit I have no business getting close to either of them.

Aiden slides a plate of scrambled eggs in front of me and I feel a bit funny on my barstool, remembering rubbing up against him during the night and hearing him groan.   I'd promised him I would keep my hands to myself.   But he'd wrapped his arms around me the moment we'd gotten into the bed, and even though we didn't have sex, the closeness and intimacy between us was greater than if we'd spent the night banging a dent into the wall with the headboard.   It's a recollection that's making me uncomfortable.

"So what do you do now?   Besides the coffeehouse thing."

"I'm an assistant professor at the community college."

"Yeah?   Archaeology?"

"Computer sciences."

Huh.   That explains the researching skills, I suppose.   I find myself dumbfounded again by the reality of him.   Aiden isn't just an asset, he's an exceptional human being - useful, helpful, just skilled enough to be necessary but all but invisible in his quiet lack of flashy proficiency.   Kaine walks in and you instantly know without any proof that he's the most dangerous man in the room.   Aiden walks in and you don't realize he's there until he's solved your problem and quietly walked back out.

Why is that suddenly so attractive to me?

"By the way, if Not Bad Earnest acts weird to you don't take it personal.   He's one of us."

"Us?"

"Yeah.   You, me, Kaine, Marta the library lady.   Earnest. We're the official Us gang now."

He thinks about it for a minute while I eat my eggs.   And then he nods, like this isn't at all a bizarre thing to be told - that your ability to see through a dimensional rift isn't in fact a break with sanity and you're now part of an exclusive club as a result.   I don't know if he's happy to be included, but he doesn't seem mad about it.

"In what capacity is Earnest an Us?"

"He's an Agent.   And something of an Ancient too, it looks like.   Hey you're gonna like this - Kaine's knocked his block off like a dozen times in the past few hundred years, like literally.   If you ever want to get under his skin just tell a decapitation joke."

The look on his face falls to something caught halfway between mortification and disbelief.

"I don't know any decapitation jokes."

"You don't?"

"I'm new to this Clarissa, I wasn't alive when beheading was in style and normal people don't generally have a ready repertoire of witty anecdotes involving head removal."

"They don't?"

The bacon is good, crispy and greasy and seared just right, and I wink at him over the strip of it hanging out of my mouth.   I can tell he doesn't know whether to take me serious or not, but it's obvious my lack of discomfort with the subject is unnerving for him.

Poor guy.

"Anyway, Mister Colin Fitzpatrick has been creeping around through history for a long time, not as long as Kaine but they crossed paths somewhere along the way - and from what I can gather it hasn't always been a peaceful relationship."   I make a neck-slicing gesture across my throat and Aiden winces a little.   "He keeps coming back, which means he's a secondlifer."

"If he's come back more than twice, wouldn't that make him a thirdlifer?"

"Naw, they just use the same word for all of it.   He'd be like an eleventhlifer by now and I'm not sure there's anybody actually keeping the books on that stuff anymore."

He's staring at my half empty plate, and I know he's coming to terms with the violent nature of what he's involved in.   I expect him to bolt at some point in the near future, but for now he seems okay with taking what comes. There's an adventurous spirit inside the overly tall, slightly thin, vaguely rumpled physicality of Aiden Magnussen. And it's a spirit I need to stay next to me for now, because Kaine has wimped out, Fitzpatrick isn't interested, and Marta is a four-foot-eleven librarian with a vision prescription in the five digits.   Aiden's what I've got to work with.

If the Genealogy section ever wakes up and joins the party again.

"He wants you."

"What?"

"Earnest...Fitzpatrick, whatever. He's got the flaming Hanes every time you walk across the room to the snack table."

"Naw, I think it's more of a professional fascination sort of thing. The Agents know about me but I've only ever met like three of them, so I'm sort of a career point for them when they come across me. Kaine's prodigy." I point to myself, but there's not any pride in my little speech. I'm just who I am. Clarissa Carmichael, human disaster with a little monster slaying on the side and a lot of personal issues.

"Yeah well...that look he gives you creeps me out. I'm telling you he's got the night sweats for you."

"There's an unwelcome mental image I could have gone a while longer without."

My phone starts buzzing as I'm finishing my juice. It's Kaine, like I knew it would be. Aiden frowns when he hears the booming deep voice and turns away to walk off, but I grab his arm to keep him where he is. This involves him.

"Get home, Clary. And bring him."

"Bring who?"

"Stoner bitch."

"I'm sorry who? There's nobody else here except one young man with an exceptional skill that you probably just realized you need. Name's Aiden. You mean him?"

There's a long angry silence and I know Kaine's hung over, cranky, and all kinds of resentful about having to say Aiden's name, especially when he knows good and well where I am right this moment.   But he does it, through gritted teeth and a reluctant acknowledgement that yeah, he sorta does need what Aiden's got to offer.   I slam my phone on the bar a few times before I hang up.

"Kaine wants us both at my place right now."

"Why?   What's going on?"

"I don't know…but he said he got a call this morning and it's a good bet that means there's been some sightings. The sort of people who call Kaine don't ring up just to say hi."

A chill shudders through me, but it's about as far from fear as a shuddery chill can get.   I'm *excited*, because after weeks of waiting for something to happen, there's finally possibly been an event.   Calls usually mean Othersiders on the wrong side of the rift.

And more exciting than that - *Kaine is back.*

I hop off my bar stool and grab my phone and jacket.   I would holler for Aiden to hurry if he wasn't already at the door, waiting for me.

Chapter Twenty Six

"Any instructions for me?"

"Yeah, don't look him directly in the eyes and don't say anything unless he asks you a question. And whatever you do, don't touch me. He's funny about people touching me." I give him a sideways look to see if he's terrified yet.

To his credit Aiden doesn't seem scared, just...annoyed. I don't think he's all that impressed with Kaine and for that I put another tally mark in his column. Stupid bravery counts for a lot in this line of work, so long as you don't get yourself killed with it.

Aiden's got a lot to live for, so I know he's going to follow the rules.

"I meant training instructions. We're being briefed for a situation containment, right? This is my first official assignment, I want to know what I'm supposed to expect."

"Oh. Well...just do as you're told, no matter how weird it sounds. It doesn't matter how much Kaine dislikes a person, as long as we're fighting on the same side he won't purposefully get you killed."

Which makes Kaine a better person that me, by a longshot.

He's waiting for us at the kitchen table when we arrive, laying out his weapons where our kids eat breakfast. He takes one look at Aiden and the cold comes into his eyes - that same cold I've seen so many times, the cold that says he's tolerating a person or a situation simply because he has no other option. It's chilling, but I'm used to it and give Aiden a shrug that he reads with surprising adeptness. He moves to the far side of the livingroom on my unspoken order, just far enough to not impose visually but still be able to hear us.

"Are the boys with Tamilla?"

A terse nod, those fiery cold blue eyes not falling anywhere near my face. He's checking his blades and I start to lay my own out; I usually have two on me just as a course of habit when getting dressed in the morning and after all these years I feel sort of naked without them. I see that he's taken the liberty of retrieving a couple of the more heavy duty weapons from my bedroom and they're laid out on the table next to his.

I don't know why that seems so intimate, but I avert my gaze for a second to get a grip on myself.

Aiden is here. Prep and dress used to turn you on but you can't be going down that road right now. No going down, period.

"Fausto brought up a valid point the other day. Tell me why we do this, Kaine."

"Tell me what his valid point was."

"I asked first - but he said we don't have any reason to be angry with them. That God was nice to them for a little while and we shouldn't have been mad about that. And now they can't reproduce anymore and there's no reason for us to be so smug about it. Or something along those lines."

Kaine goes silent, and it's in that long stretch without words that the truth lies simmering.

"He's right. They only ever reacted to the way they were treated. Their punishment never sat right with me...but neither did mine."

"Which means what?"

"Which means they never should have been sent across in the first place. But it's done and the person who did it isn't taking calls as of just about a half a millennia ago." He reaches under the table and brings out a carefully wrapped weapon whose shape I recognize before he's even untied the blanket obscuring it.

The ramba. This is more serious than I thought. But my head is still hovering over what he just said, and the fact that he included himself in the punishment part is dragging hard at my tongue and I'm having a hard time holding back from blurting out what's forming in my head. He's not entirely on board with why we do what we do. But he *is* entirely on board with doing it anyway.

"How long have you felt like this?"

"I don't have feelings, Clary. You know that. I do what I'm meant to do and I don't question it, and I sure as hell don't feel one way or the other about it."

"But you said their punishment never sat right with you - "

"I have a sense of justice, Clary. No heart, but my head still works."

He's mad, I know. He's also tired and he's hurt and he's regretting a stupidly long lifetime of enforcing policies he may not have ever truly believed in and he's probably *really* pissed off to be in the same room with Aiden, but the simple fact that he's laid the ramba on the table means

186

he's swallowed all that he knows is wrong and is now solidly digging in to duty.

And...oh god, he's moved away from the table and started strapping on the leathers.

This is the part I truly can't help - when Kaine armors up I don't just go weak in the knees, I go damp in the Hanes For Her.   Those low-slung black leather pants might or might not be the reason for our oldest child and potentially our youngest as well, if I'm being honest.   And though there's a little more of him hanging over the waistband than there used to be, for an old guy he's still shockingly fit.

Kaine might be ancient, but he's still got it.

A third child is the last thing in the world I could possibly want at this point in my life though, and Aiden is still lurking somewhere in visual distance, so I drag my eyes off the rock hard hills and stone smooth planes of Kaine's bare chest and try to saddle my concentration onto the skittish horse of the task at hand.   It's the same task that's always at hand, and we both know I'm never going to let it go. But one day we'll march into our final battle, and I fully intend to have my answer before I can no longer ask for it...or he can no longer give it.

"How old, Kaine."

He sighs, but it sounds different this time, slightly off from the usual resigned emptying of lungs that I've been listening to for the last thirty plus years every time I ask.   This time it sounds like a final gasp.

He's on the rails, I can feel it.   He's told me about battles and wars that have been hinted at in mythology but that nobody's really sure actually happened.   He's crossed paths with historical figures whose timelines can be dated but it's always with a condescending tone that he tells the tale, like he was the adult watching an inexperienced kid make history-changing mistakes.   I know he's older than everyone in his stories.   Sometimes it feels like he's older than everyone on the planet.

"I've been doing this for - "

"No, I didn't ask how long you've been doing it.   I asked how old you are.   We all might die today and I don't want to go out never having gotten an answer out of you."   He looks up from where he's been buckling his chest strap and squints at me.   But it isn't his intimidating squint.   It's his *Goddammit Clary* squint, and it's always meant I've pestered him just about enough.

I hear Aiden clear his throat from somewhere over by the door and although I know he probably stopped listening somewhere around *We all might die today*, to his immense credit he's keeping his mouth shut and not asking any questions.   He also hasn't headed for the exit yet, and for that I owe him my undying gratitude and a couple shots of the good stuff...because if I'd heard what came next without a witness to back me up, I might be tempted to doubt it ever happened.

Doubt isn't in my nature though.   Look at what I am - I've been accepting the most twisted facts in human history without question for just about my entire life, so what comes next only skips across my belief system for about a second and a half before it settles into gospel.

"Six thousand seven hundred and thirty two."   There's a heavy sigh to follow the resigned one as Kaine leans over and puts his fists on the table, supporting his weight against them.   "Give or take."

Mental math isn't my strong point, but I do remember my Biblical history, twisted as it's been through my own. "You're joking.   That would put you in the same timeline as the Garden of Eden."

"Nice place, if you can get past the sword-spinning nightmares posted at the front gate."

"What - you're serious?"

And then it comes to me, a slap in the head so stinging and brain-rattling that all I can do is stare at him, slack jawed and stuck somewhere between *Ohmygod this is incredible* and *Holy shit I hope this isn't true.*   Because there's something that's been bugging me for a few decades, and it's taking a form now that looks disconcertingly real.

"Please tell me you're not the original Cain."

He doesn't look at me.

"I've always been a hunter, Clary.   Somewhere along the way I just switched prey."

CHAPTER TWENTY SEVEN

"But...that would make you one of the first humans.   Are you saying..."

I know the next words out of my mouth are going to be some of the most ludicrous I've ever spoken, but it's shaping up to be one of those mornings.   *"You were one of Adam and Eve's kids?"*

He's still not looking at me, but even without the benefit of eye contact I know he's speaking the truth.   For one, there's much better lies he could be telling, and for two, there's absolutely no reason to doubt him.   I've been to the Sistine Chapel, I know whose face that is at the center of The Final Judgement.   He huffs out a derisive little laugh completely devoid of humor but still, somehow, peckishly amused.   "First generation of the natural borns."

"So Adam was your daddy."

"Afraid so.   I was the first family disappointment."

I'll say.   Goddamn.   I always wanted an answer but now that I've got it, I'm not sure how to process it.   "You...you killed your brother.   *That* Cain, that's who we're talking about here?   The *first killer*.   The first to spill blood on the new Earth.   The guy who figured out that life was finite and proved it and got put in the Bible as a cautionary tale for being a rage filled dick with temper control issues. That was *you*."

"Why do you think I was cursed with eternal life and an unbendable edict to hunt monsters until the end of it all?"

I can hear Aiden shuffling his feet nervously from across the room but I can't be bothered with checking on him right now.   I've got Kaine giving answers to questions that are older than him, and frankly at this moment he's on his own because I'm not stopping.   Not while Kaine is talking.   I know he's going to close up shop on the answer factory soon and whatever I can get from him before he sulls up, you better believe I'm going to get.

"You mean God was like 'If you like killing so much, here, now you have to do it for the rest of your life, which oh by the way, that's *forever* baby'?   Was it like that?   Because I'm imagining it was like that."

"Pretty much, yeah."

"Oh my god."

There's an odd sort of sadness mixed with what I can only call impotent rage in Kaine's face, and his next words verify my suspicions.   He's good at what he does because it's what he's always been.   *He invented killing.*   And he's perfected it to an art that nobody else in the whole world can even come close to.

"I understand monsters, Clary.   I was the first monster."

Holy shit, there it is.   Not only why he does it, but why he does it so well.   He's self aware, which removes him just about a step from the serial killers who have followed in his path over the centuries.   This man wrote the book.

I actually feel bad for him.   I'm mortified and appalled at what he did to earn his curse, but it seems a bit extreme in the long run.   Six thousand plus years of hunting monsters...monsters whose birth he witnessed himself. Because if his numbers are accurate - and I know they are - he was there when it all began.   And his curse is to be there when it all ends.

"You were there when the Abominations started, weren't you.   Are they who I think they are?"

"Yes."

It seems that's all he's going to say on the matter, and I'm surprisingly okay with it.   The tragic tale of how the vampires, werewolves, sea monsters, ghosts and ghouls and trolls and every other dark-walking demon ever dreamed up in the feverish nightmares of mankind came into existence - I know where they came from, I don't need to hear it from Kaine now that I have confirmation. Anyone with a basic biblical knowledge, no matter how they view the truth or fiction of the book itself, knows.   It's there in black and white, a basic hardline fact to the fanciful stories people tell around the campfire, of the cursed creatures Stoker and Poe and Shelley and Romero wrote about. There's no fiction to any of it.

They were writing history, not horror.

"The monsters we slay now, they're the descendants of the first wave of angels that left heaven to mate with the humans," Kaine says quietly. "The Nephilim were the first once the genetics started breaking down...or powering up, whichever way you prefer to look at it. Giants. The first legends, the first godless gods to walk the earth." He's turning the ramba in his hands, which makes me nervous. That thing's got mental issues and doesn't react well to being touched, but Kaine's been its master for as long as I've known him and I know it can sense his thoughts. So long as he stays calm we'll all be fine. "Every generation after that just became more and more of an abomination until the rift was created and they were all banished to the other side of it. Banished to protect what was intended for the light of day. The *good* ones."

Aiden coughs nervously somewhere to my right. He seems closer, but I don't check to see if he's moved. I can't bear the thought of the look I know has to be on his face right about now.

"They didn't deserve it, did they?" Fausto's words are bouncing around in my head, echoing with that strange sort of angry sadness that had crept ominously through his voice. "They're the maker's children just like everyone else, if they're related to the angels. Maybe more so, right? I mean...mankind isn't even *in* that family tree, and the angels are higher up in the creationary line...if the Othersiders are descendants of the angels then they're closer to God than we are."

Kaine nods, that ramba still turning slowly in his hands. It's then that I remember it's a vengeance weapon. It shouldn't be in the gear we're prepping unless he's got more than just negotiations in mind.

"True, they are. But they weren't a direct creation like normal man was. They were something else...a deviation...half what they were meant to be, and half what they weren't."

"That wasn't by choice though. Aren't they being punished for what the fallen angels did? Because it sounds like they got saddled paying forever for something God's *own direct creation* did wrong and that's sort of pissing me off, Kaine."

He's eyeing the business edge of the blade while it hums threateningly in his grip, singing its deadly little song of mayhem in tune with the words he's speaking. "That's about the size of it. They weren't granted the right of prayer, to talk to their maker like the rest of humanity was welcome to do. Couldn't petition their own case. They rebelled, of course. Did terrible things, getting their revenge on the favored side of creation every chance they got.   Creeping around in the shadows murdering and maiming and terrifying the innocents, creating stories that followed them through history."   He finally puts the cursed blade down on the table and brings his eyes to mine, and they're dark with a rage I know he's been carrying for thousands of years.   "Dracula, the werewolf, the mummy...fairies and zombies and trolls and fucking Frankenstein.   It was all them.   So the line was drawn and they were banished to the other side of it.   And we protect this side, because that line doesn't always hold."

"Fuck."

It takes both of us a full several seconds to realize that the word didn't come from either of us, and we look over at Aiden, standing there staring into nothing with a mortified look on his face.   It's undoubtedly a lot to process for a newcomer and I wish he could be included in the discussion, but Kaine is tolerating his presence based on a very strict set of conditions that I know I can't breach.   We go back to ignoring him, but I make a mental note to take him out for a glass of the good stuff if we make it past this afternoon alive.

Maybe Kaine will join us.

"But...your brother..."

"Yeah."

I don't want to throw any more guilt on him than I know he's already hefting around on that strong back of his, but there's something I've got to know.

"Does it ever freak you out that we have two boys?"

"All the damn time."

"So every time they fight you're internally panicking that one of them is going to take a rock to the other one's head."

"Shut up Clary."

"And I'll tell you right now, I know which one it's gonna be because that little one has a temper like a drunk badger -
"

"Shut up Clary."

The moment is broken, the heaviness and dark tragedy lightened to a bearable level by Kaine's embarrassment at being called out.   That's when I glance over toward the livingroom and meet eyes with Aiden.   He's been standing there silently through what has got to be the weirdest conversation he's ever had to listen to, taking it all in, sorting it in his head, drawing his own conclusions about what we are and whether or not he wants to be a part of it in light of this new set of facts.   The look on his face makes me feel a little bit sick - because that's exactly how he looks, like what he just heard is sitting hard and heavy on his stomach and he'd like nothing better than to throw up and be rid of it.

I know how he feels.   But it's like Kaine has always said to me - I've got the stomach of a slayer, and even though my heart is crying at the injustice of it all, my hands are reaching for my weapons.   Because regardless of how the whole thing started, it's ended up being what it is, and what it is is dangerous and bloody and full of all the bad things that absolutely have to be kept out of the world.

I don't know if Kaine made me who I am or if this has always been me and he simply found me and made use of me.   Either way, I don't like the fact that I'm about to follow him willingly into a battle that should never have been provoked.

But here we are.

(HAPTER TWENTY EIGHT

"Well if it isn't the Macedonian.   How you doin' oldtimer?"

"No one has called me that in a very long time."

"Yeah, well - there's not a lot of us left who remember what went down, all those years ago, across the sea...how's the old home place these days?"

Kaine narrows his eyes and I know they're speaking a private language that only the two of them understand. Their past is a point of contention and whatever happened in Macedonia is a very sore spot between them, that much is clear.

"I wouldn't know.   I haven't been back in a while."

"Yeah that's right, you got kicked out didn't you.   You know, I think that'd just about make me nuts, not being able to go back to the place I call home..."   Fausto goes silent, letting his words hang heavy in the dimly lit room, the irony and sarcasm settling like lead.   "Oh yeah, that's right, I can't.   Guess that makes me nuts then.   And so are all my kit and kin on the other side of that line."   He leans forward, all menace and threat but with eyes only for Kaine.   "You should step very lightly here, old man."

"I'm not the one who put you there."

"But you're the one who kept us there, aren't you Kaine. You made it your life's work to make sure all of us abominations in the eyes of the maker stayed put nice and quiet in a dark place where we couldn't even make families for ourselves.   Ain't that right."   The big man drags his eyes over to me, finally seeming to notice there's someone here besides his nemesis.   "His name used to be *Prokolnat Branitel* back then.   That's what the people called him during the big uprising back in what, 925 or so? AD, BC, I forget what era.   Fuck all that, it's just dark on our side, we don't mark days because there aren't any."   He turns his head toward the window, those mismatched eyes closing slowly like a cat basking in a warm morning windowsill even though there's barely any sun coming in. "Prokolnat Branitel…it means Cursed Defender.   Even those backwards peasants knew, eh Kaine?"

"Fausto, we have bad blood between us but I'm here to warn you that your people will suffer unless you cross back and stay where you belong."

"Where we *belong*?   Really, Kaine?   And don't you belong in hell?   Doesn't look like you stayed there."

There's a long pause during which I know at least four hands are moving slowly toward the weapons made for them and that all it will take is one shift in tone, one quick move, one misinterpreted flinch and every hidden blade will instantly be on the clock.   But Fausto's tone stays calm and even, and the only movement in the room is Aiden's chest rising and falling just a little bit too rapidly with his breathing.   A panic attack would be unfortunate and potentially catastrophic right about now and I look over at him, raising an eyebrow in assessment of his current nervous health.

He shakes his head.   Poor guy's doing his best, but the truth is he's an assistant computer sciences professor, not a warrior...and it's never been more painfully obvious than it is at this moment.   He's not a slayer.   And he's only here pretending to be one because of me.

I know I can't live with his death on my conscience.   If there's a throwdown here today, I'm going to be split between doing my job and keeping him alive, and I'm not even sure if that makes me anxious or just irritated.   Aiden should be on recon or emergency backup somewhere outside this room, not standing here ten feet from the rift beside the deadliest slayer in history and me, staring in something like awestruck fascination at the source of all nightmares.

Something's really gone off the rails with protocol lately, and the fact that Kaine's allowed it unnerves me more than just a little bit.

And then Fausto starts talking again and it's all for Kaine, the rest of us might as well not even be in the room. "Oh yeah, you never actually *went* to hell, did you. Struck a deal with God, agreed to hunt us in exchange for not roasting eternity away in the bad place. Am I telling this right?"

Something flinches in Kaine's face but he doesn't say anything. He told me once that there was no hell or else he'd have been in it. I know now that he's been in it all along, and he's the only one there.

"I'm warning you, Fausto. Go back across and stay there. I'm not here to negotiate, I'm here to toss your pieces through that rift if you don't do as you're told."

"Toss my pieces." The big werewolf laughs and I can see his sharp teeth even in the dim light. "Do. As. I. Am. *Told.* Your accent never has gotten any better, has it old man? Never really grasped the lay of the language either. You spent way too long in Scotland speakin' that Gaelic shit - but I have to hand it to you, Clarissa here - " He points at me dismissively. "She's impressed me. She comes in here acting like she's about two feet taller and eighty pounds heavier than what I'm lookin' at and she stands up to me and my Uncle like a natural born slayer, just her and that boy over there. And I thought she was, at first. You know, a real slayer.   But then I figured out who she is, and damned if I'm not a little bit sick to my stomach at the thought of her being with you all this time."

I'm just about to ask *What's he talking about?* when Kaine spins around and slams into the big werewolf with his left elbow, the crash of the thick joint hitting Fausto's eye socket making a hideous sound that has always reminded me of ice floes cracking in Antarctica documentaries. Fausto staggers back about three steps and then shakes it off, his shaggy long hair flying like a dog coming in from the rain.   There's a deep ragged curse uttered and it's obvious that elbow hurt.

"Are we doin' this, old man?"   There's blood dribbling slowly from Fausto's nose and the tip of his tongue snakes out to lick it away.

"Aye, we are."

Those giant shoulders shrug dismissively, and the look on the feral face is no more concerned than a man who's just been told it's time for dinner.   "Okay then."

I wish I could say I knew exactly what happened in the seconds that followed. I know that Kaine and Fausto squared off and that the big Othersider was the first to throw an official punch, signaling the chaos that flared into confusing life within seconds of his fist making contact with the back of Kaine's head. He had turned to see where I was and Fausto had taken advantage of that split second moment when his eyes weren't on him. It was a hell of a blow and I heard Aiden suck in a sympathy breath at the exact same time I did.

That was pretty much when it all went to hell. A blinding flash blasts through the room like a minor nuclear event and just like that, the rift blows open and we're standing there, exposed, in the full presence of an open doorway to the Other Side.

Even I can see it this time.

"Is he useful??"

I look where Kaine's pointing and groan; Aiden is standing by the door looking like the last person you'd pick for dodge ball. It's not that he seems incapable, he's just very obviously confused and astounded at the scene around him, and neither Kaine nor myself have the time at the moment to explain any of it to him. I shake my head and hold up my blade, signaling that this is what we've got to work with and the rest are just casualties waiting to hit the floor. Kaine rolls his eyes and turns back to Fausto, and as his long coat settles behind him I see the shape of the ramba hilt underneath it.

He brought the big guns.   I never saw him take it off the table, but since he did it can only mean he's operating on the assumption that someone in this room will be a bigger challenge than expected, because that ramba's been in the weapons vault since our tenth anniversary and I never actually thought I'd see the thing again.   It has imprinting abilities, a hell of an advantage in a fight where you're surrounded.

Like now.   The rift has spread to encompass all of section J and at least five Othersiders have tentatively stepped through, looking around, obviously not sure if they should be here.   Which tells me Fausto didn't plan this - armaggeddon or whatever he's got cooking isn't on the calendar for today.   I step in front of one of the abominations and give him a nasty look and he freezes, staring at me with wide amber eyes that look more scared than malevolent.   He's a FaeGhoul.   Nasty in the best of situations, but he's not showing any aggression and I think he's just as caught off guard by all of this as we are.

"Is this the battlefield you want your name on in the history books?" I ask him, holding up my tanto.   His nervous stare goes to it and he shakes his head slowly before turning his attention to Fausto and Kaine.   The head shake gets more decisive then and I know he hasn't followed the big werewolf across to be part of the coup.   He just wandered out because it was open.   The one behind him seems to feel the same way.   "Go back over and you'll be fine. This - "   I wave a hand toward the two idiots going fist to fist by section H - "This is personal.   No need to get involved."

The FaeGhoul seems relieved to be excused from the festivities and quietly retreats back toward the rift, taking two of the other arrivees with him.   Three others stay and I keep my eyes on them; at least one of them sends a shiver up my spine and the way he's watching Kaine puts me on full alert.   It's a shapeshifter, nervously changing colors like he can't control himself.

"A little help?" Kaine grunts from his currently untenable position, on his knees facing away from the gigantic werewolf crouched behind him.   Fausto's forearm, thick as a tree trunk, is cutting off his air supply at the throat and Kaine's face is starting to take on a disconcertingly bluish hue.   He's got one hand out toward me, fingers grasping to indicate he wants my tanto.

"No way, use the ramba."

Fausto's eyes narrow when that word reaches his ears and I can see something like panic flit quickly across his face. Kaine just looks at me like I blew his cover in a particularly riveting round of hide and seek and now, with his ass hanging out, he's got no choice but to run like hell for base.

"You've got a fucking *ramba?*"

Fausto obviously wants none of that but he isn't letting go of Kaine's throat; going for the weapon would be pointless and he knows it.   Ramba tech is old and sloppy and if he touches the cursed blade it'll imprint on him, making him its sole target until the day it shoves its way through his heart or takes off his head.   I've seen it do both and it's not something I want to mess with either, even though technically I'm on the safe list - but the Ancients who built it were likely drunk off their asses on fermented cranberries and as a result of their passing out in the middle of laying the curse on it, the stupid thing has a tendency to get confused.   The only being that's been able to wield it properly since its creation is the man who's currently on his knees and starting to choke in the grip of a pissed off half blind Other.

"Not looking good, Kaine" I chastise him on my way to the door.   He pulls a hand away from Fausto's massive forearm and flips me off as I stroll out, Aiden following behind me like a confused puppy that isn't sure which yard it belongs in.   The looks on those FaeGhouls' faces told me everything I need to know - and that's that this fight shouldn't be happening.   We've got no reason to be here, armed to the eyelids, making threats and acting tough. Someone crossed the line and let themselves be seen on the east end of town?   Scared some elderly shopkeeper that was locking up for the night?   Okay, yes, they're not allowed to do that...but knocking on their front door with an arsenal left over from the Dark Ages is a bit heavyhanded and I didn't hear anyone on our side asking politely if they could keep their kids off our lawn.

Whatever happens in there, I'm not going to be a part of it. It's obvious at this point that it's personal, and if there's one thing I know to be gospel, it's that you don't get in the middle of a blood grudge.

"Shouldn't we help him?" Aiden asks as the heavy door falls shut behind us.

"You got any ideas on how to do that?"

The confusion that's been etched into his face for the last ten minutes just goes deeper and he hesitates while the door swings on its weighted hinges, slowing down each time it hits its apex.   By the time it's still, he's made his decision.

"He brought us for backup."

"Aiden, he's not in any danger."

"You said that thing is an Ancient...whatever."

"Yeah, and so is Kaine.   Trust me, they're just going to roll around like a couple of high school boys in the dirt until they get tired and agree to continue later.   It's what they do.   And if things get critical, Kaine's armed out the wazoo."

"But there are more of them.   I saw them.   There were dozens on the other side watching."

"All the more reason for me to get you out of here, pretty boy."

I take two steps before I realize the swinging door is swinging again, and my pretty boy is on the other side of it, headed straight for Fausto and Kaine.

What followed is something I won't be forgetting any time soon, mainly because of the look on my ex husband's face when the skinny hippie he wrote off as a liability marched up to the pair of them with Volume S-T of the Encyclopedia Brittanica clutched in his hands and swung it.   But it didn't connect with Fausto's head, as one would expect in an interference event where an oversized foe has an unfair advantage and a third party is wielding a stupid big book. No, he walked up and clocked Kaine square in the face, and the second Kaine went limp in that brief eyeblink moment when the blow of 1,986 pages and a thick resinboard cover reset his brain to zero, Fausto's grip released in surprise.

And Kaine, like Kaine is known to do, recovered his wits in the very next blink and spun around with a leg out to sweep Fausto's feet out from under him.

It was a beautiful move all around - a little bit messy and not at all by the book unless you wanted to take the literal route - and as Aiden stepped back out of the way, the two Ancients resumed their battle on a more even keel. Suddenly I didn't know which I wanted to do more...kiss that tall skinny blessing in disguise or take that encyclopedia to the side of his head for declaring himself every bit as big of an idiot as the pair of them.

I opt for giving him a quick nod of approval as we vacate the battleground together. Best not to incapacitate your allies before the fight is over. There's always time for that later.

CHAPTER TWENTY NINE

Kaine doesn't talk to me for about a week - but Fausto does. I guess watching me abandon the king of the slayers on the battlefield without a backward glance awakened some kind of a realization in the old werewolf that I'm someone who can be reasoned with, and though werewolves aren't typically the reasonable sort, that's the route he decides to take. I can only guess that he sweet talked one of the research assistants into getting my number from the library card records, maybe even placing the call herself.

I'll own up to being possessed of a mighty bone-shaking chill when I hear that voice coming through my phone.

"Come talk to me, Clarissa. You know where to find me."

He didn't say to come alone, so I don't - thirty years of dealing with the most deviously underhanded creatures to ever walk the shadows has taught me several unimpeachable truths, the first being that you can never trust an Othersider and do not think for one second that this one will be different.

Nothing about Fausto instills either trust or complacency in me.   But there's something about that gigantic Ancient that makes me anxious to hear what he has to say despite all the alarms that should be blaring in my head, and I tuck my tanto into the back of my yoga pants on my way out the door because safety first, more safety second.   The kids are in school, Kaine is god knows where, and Aiden has been summarily texted and instructed to meet me on the front steps of the library for a quick briefing.   The whole thing could easily go sideways, and something deep inside some insidious little corner of my psyche sorta hopes it will.

Which is why I'm arming Aiden, and hoping for the best.

"Is this that ramba thing?   I don't want that thing, it scares the bejeezus out of me.   Kaine stole it off Vampire Hunter D didn't he?"

"It's not the ramba.   You really think I'd hand you an imprint weapon that lost its mind somewhere around the sixth century and has been hunting on its own for the last two hundred years?   It's sentient, Aiden.   You don't ever get to touch it because trust me, it'll sense your fear and skewer you just for the fun of hearing you scream like a little girl."

He stares at me, squinting hard against the mid morning sun, his face all twisted up adorably.   We'd jumped each other's bones immediately following the incident with the encyclopedia, but we've managed to keep it in our pants for the last few days since then - which is pointless really, since Kaine doesn't want anything to do with me. Something about watching your ex wife walk out while you're getting your ass handed to you by an Othersider seems to have a dampening effect on emotional attachment.   Maybe he's really done with me this time.

That would probably be ideal, but I doubt I can get that lucky.

"So this one isn't going to turn on me?"   Aiden's holding up the knife I just handed him, eyeing it distrustfully.   "It's not alive, right?   If it's all the same to you I'd rather have something *not* possessed by Jack the Ripper."

I reach out and shove his hand down, taking a quick scan of the parking lot to verify that no one is watching us and calling the police to report a couple outside the library brandishing knives.   "You're good, that one's just got the soul of Diego Deza in it.   So long as you stay away from fire you should be fine."

I can tell his brain is racing around trying to figure out where he knows that name from, and while he's sorting it I head into the library and leave him standing there. Fausto's waiting for me and you don't keep a werewolf waiting if you want to walk out the same way you walked in - with all your limbs attached and your heart still in your chest. This one is a fleshrender, he wouldn't think twice about taking a bite out of me for rudeness.

Aiden is beside me before I realize it. He's taking his job seriously, an endearing trait in a sidekick. I remind him that he's only here for backup and that he's to stay out of the way, not speak, and blend as inconspicuously into the nondescript beige walls of the corridor as possible, with his phone in one hand and the hilt of that borrowed knife in the other. He doesn't like it, but he nods his agreement and I know he's going to obey me. That foolhardy move with the encyclopedia might have gotten him laid in a lusty near-death frenzy last time, but if he tries it again I've put it to him in no uncertain terms that I'll kill him myself - and there will be no sex involved until after he's dead and I've left his corpse at the mouth of the rift for Fausto's kind to play with as they see fit.

I have no doubt he believes me.

Fausto meets us at the door to the Genealogy section, those unnerving mismatched eyes going from me to Aiden and back to me with an amused quirk that all but points and bursts out laughing at my hastily arranged backup plan. He obviously doesn't think much of my partner. Which is good, because it's almost always the ones you underestimate who end up putting something pointy into your aorta while you're busy assuming they're harmless.

Aiden *is* harmless, mostly. But I know what he has at risk here, and as a psychotically protective parent myself I know it won't take much to turn him deadly in one way or another.

Without a word Fausto nods and turns to go into the little room where the rift is humming, singing its oddly off-key little tune that seems to be getting louder each time I'm near it. The last time we saw it it was open wide enough for Othersiders to step through without much difficulty; this time it's mostly closed but flapping strangely, almost like there's a stiff breeze blowing through it. I can see the tangible shimmer, but from the way Aiden is staring wide-eyed I know he's seeing way more than I am.

I don't have time to waste asking him about it.

"Stay out here. Don't come in under any circumstances, you clear? If things go south call Kaine."

Aiden nods, pulling his eyes away from the rift with some difficulty.   There's nothing in his face that implies any resentment at being relegated to Get Help status.   This is a man who knows his best fighting skill is in getting somebody who can fight.

You gotta respect that.

Fausto gets right down to it, launching into his commentary before he's even turned around to face me.

"Do you remember Kaine's last wife before you?"   He cocks that cracked brow while he's saying it and I know he's not really asking me anything, he's just setting up the next part of his story in the way he figures will catch my attention the most.   "Of course you don't, it was about a hundred and fifty years before you were born.   But did he ever tell you what happened to her?"

"She was mortal, I'm assuming he just outlived her."

"Oh yeah, he outlived her alright.   Just like he outlived *all* of his wives and kids.   That's the shitty thing about not dying...everybody else just can't help doing it."

My head jumps around looking for the reason behind this particular line of conversation.   Is he trying to distract me? Kaine's nearly seven thousand years old, he's had more wives, lovers, families than I'd care to count and I'd be stupid if I bothered to get jealous over any of it.   I'm one in

216

a long distinguished line, I know.   I also know I won't be the last, if I can manage to keep him alive through the next thirty or so years.

"Is there a point to this?   Because A, I know Kaine's had a lot of wives over the centuries, why wouldn't he?   And B, I need a coffee real damn bad and you're cutting into the fifteen minutes I have allotted to get to the Starbucks on Main before lunchtime traffic hits, so lets move this along please."

That arresting stare moves past me and I know he's checking Aiden's position in the corridor.   He no doubt remembers that impressive swing that knocked the stars right out of Kaine's skull the last time we were all in the same room together.   There's not a chance in hell he's nervous about Aiden being here, but a good warrior never gives even the enemy's waterboy the opportunity to sneak up behind him.

"I killed Kaine's last wife.   Elise, that was her name.   I always remember the names that go with the hearts I eat." Those long fangs seem longer suddenly and it's all I can do not to take a step back, reorient myself quickly, choose a spot to dig into and defend...because this giant fleshrender is showing his teeth and naming names of the deceased, and that's never a good omen.   But I stand my ground and force an internal stand-down simply because he hasn't moved toward me yet, and his hands are still hanging empty at his sides.   "Pretty Lithuanian girl, dark hair, light eyes.   From what I understand Kaine jumped off the roof of the Maison de Lac with her on his back and her baby in his arms during the fuckstorm of 1802 with a pike through his left shoulder and half blind from cedar ash burns.   Cedar, that's what they used against us back in the day.   Sets fire to our lungs from the inside, it's a nasty way to die.   We call that the Night of Blood and Tears now, you may have heard about it.   Kaine was the big hero of that battle...at least officially."

Yeah, I've heard about it.   Massive casualties on both sides of that one.   And I know about Elise, though Kaine never talks about his past wives and families much.

"I still don't hear a point being made."

"I killed her for revenge.   Kaine and his crew slaughtered half my clan that night.   I mean yeah, all's fair in love and war and baby that was a hell of a war.   But Kaine and I, we've been fucking each other across the centuries for a long damn time now.   And at the moment, he's one up on me."

There's a menacing look in his eyes as he speaks that last sentence, leaning toward me as if he's about to share some dark secret.

"He got me back.   You know what he did?"

I shake my head, a creeping dread in my gut telling me I probably don't want to hear this.

"He stole one of my pups."

Gut was right.   I didn't want to hear that.

"Kids are off limits.   Always have been.   Kaine wouldn't do that."

"True that, babydoll.   But he did.   Trespassed across the line into my world and snatched one of my young ones, right out of the den.   My tiny one."   He cocks his head to one side and I'm called to mind of a great big shaggy dog, right in that nervous moment when you can't guess whether or not he's about to take a bite at you.   "She was named Clarissa too.   Imagine that."

There's something that sounds like a gasp from behind me, and just about the time it dawns on me that Aiden has grasped something I haven't, it hits me.

CHAPTER THIRTY

It would have been less of a shock if he had taken a bite at me.

"You better have something to back that up, if you're claiming what I think you are."

"Have you ever felt like you were losing your damn mind when the moon goes full, like it's talking to you but you can't sort out what it's saying?   Like you used to speak the language but somehow you forgot it."

"That's a bad combo of PMS and schizophrenia, only one of which I'll own up to having."

He laughs.   He hasn't said it yet.   As long as he doesn't say it I won't have to think about it, and if I don't think about it I won't have to acknowledge that yeah, me and the moon, we have this thing.   It's always been like that, a deep and abiding obsession - and slaying suits me so well partly because most of it's done by the light of the moon. I always sort of thought that was why I liked being out at night so much, because that silvery glow in the middle of the sky meant it was time to go to work.

And god I loved the work.

But it's not a confirmation by any means, and so far he's not backing up the insinuation that's laying there between us, still and quiet, waiting for a blast of lightning to send life coursing through it like the scarfaced twisted beast it is.

She was named Clarissa too.   Imagine that.

But I don't have a monopoly on the name, so it's not a given yet.

Yet.

So we stand there in silence, him with words he needs me to hear, me wondering if a quick prayer for spontaneous muteness would fall on deaf ears.   Because I know in my bones that there isn't going to be a lot of doubt in me once he speaks the words he's holding onto behind the oddly hopeful smugness of that snaggletoothed grin.

Why am I like this?

You're a slayer, Clary.   Same as me.

Yeah but you were made this way, weren't you?   My mom and dad go to church, they don't believe in ghosts, they made me play with dolls.   I wasn't born a slayer.

And what did you do to those dolls, Clary?   Did you dress them up pretty or did you behead them and pull their arms and legs off?   You're like me, sweetheart...we don't belong to either side.   We're the middle.   We're something else.

Are we the good guys?

Kaine had fallen silent for so long that I'd assumed he wasn't going to answer me, staring off across the rooftops at the black sky that stretched out forever.

We do what we're told is right, Clary.   That's what we do. We just...we do our best.

Fausto's deep rumbling voice drags me back to the room we're standing in.

"You're one of mine, Clarissa.   Kaine stole you to get back at me for Elise.   He took you when you were too young to know what you were and put you with a human family so you'd grow up as one of them.   And then when you were old enough, he took you and made you a slayer.   Turned you against your own kind, made you hunt your own people.   And then he sent you after me."

There it is.   I couldn't ask for it to be more plain and concise and to the point if I'd personally requested for him to make it all three.

You're one of mine.   Kaine stole you.

He took you.

He made you a slayer.

In that short selection of words Fausto has answered nearly every question I've ever asked Kaine.   And there's nothing there, not one word, that isn't a bright and shining testament to honesty.   I can feel it.   And now that he's said it, nothing in me has any desire to dispute it.   Kaine has always told me that if something settles into you the moment you hear it spoken and nothing in you screams that it's a lie, then it's a truth - *your* truth - and you better just accept it as nothing but.

Fausto has just spoken my truth, and there's not a whisper of disagreement in me anywhere.

Truth is sort of like that.

"I've never changed."

It's a weak argument and I know it - and Fausto knows it too, because he tilts his head and gives me a look with *You know better than that* scrawled all over it.   And he's right, I do know better.   It's one of the basic truths of the monsters, that there are more of their kind on this side than anyone knows.   That Othersiders who've forgotten who they are - or never truly knew to begin with - live and look just like everyone else over here.

I could live my entire life never knowing.   Because it's the rift, the other side of the line, that tells us what we are.

223

And in all my years of fighting everything that lives on the other side of it, I've never, not once, stepped across that line.

I haven't been allowed to.   Kaine has always kept me carefully away from it, told me that one day I'd have to cross over and fight on their territory but till then just trust him that it's not a place I want to go.

I've been there, he'd said.

And I've always done just that - trusted him and stayed clear.   I'm standing closer to the dividing line right now than I've ever been in my thirty plus years of fighting everything that's dared to step out of it, and I know things now that I woke up this morning not knowing.   I know them deep inside, where lies can't survive and only truth has form.   And the form this one particular truth is taking is a surprising sense of calm.

I'd love to analyze it, but he's talking again.

"That boy that comes with you.   I can see it when he looks at you.   Boy loves you."

I feel my head shake involuntarily at the sudden shift in subjects.   Fausto's looking past me again and I hope to god Aiden's still obeying me, staying in the corridor and out of reach of everything that's in this room with me.   This cursed Othersider is claiming to be my dad but I don't trust him any further than I can hurl my blade even though I know he's telling the truth.   Paternity doesn't equal

224

harmless in either of our worlds.   And though any normal person would probably be shocked, appalled, mortified at what I just found out...I'm none of it.

Mostly I'm just sort of numb.

I glance back over my shoulder.   Aiden's at the door, technically still outside the room but much closer than I want him.   With the sparking light from the rift reflecting off his face he reminds me of Morpheus standing over someone's nightmare.

I turn back to Fausto.   "Boy is a lot younger than me.   A lot."

"So?   He stood up to me.   He looked right into the rift, saw what was in it, and didn't run.   He stayed by you. You could do worse, Clarissa.   Hell, you *have* done worse. Motherfucking *Kaine*."

"Yeah well, nobody told me he had a blood feud with the leader of the Other Side before I married him, though to be honest I always sort of felt like I was probably adopted. My parents were religious and I ended up hunting monsters."

"Hey, Van Helsing worked for the Vatican."

I can't argue with that - movies get it right more often than you'd think.   He moves a little bit closer and his voice drops to a soft cadence that seems oddly, disconcertingly familiar.

"We just want to be in the light, Clarissa. It's where we came from. That kind over there decided we came from the dark and that's where we needed to be banished back to. Bullshit. Did you know we came from heaven? Nothing but warm light...our ancestors were angels..."

He's closer now, and I know I should be backing up to stay beyond his reach. For some stupid reason I don't, and while I stand my ground he slowly advances until I can feel his breath against my face.

"I don't see what any of this has to do with me. Why did you call me here?"

"You were my only little girl Clarissa. All your brothers, they're all dead now. Most of them killed by Kaine. You're all that's left of us. We can't reproduce over here anymore, that all stopped decades ago. We're dying."

No...no no no. No. I get the really sick feeling I know where this line of conversation is headed and I'm not going there under any circumstances. Blood or no blood, last of the line or not, Fausto's not getting my kids.

I don't draw a lot of lines, but I'm drawing one here, and I will die on it if I have to.

"Either you come to the point or I'm taking my stoner bitch and going home."

His eyes drop to some point south of my throat and for a moment, just a brief handful of seconds, I feel like I might actually be in serious trouble.   Fausto is a Master.   And even though I've been trained for decades by Kaine - also a Master - there are certain facts inherent in being me that I can't deny...the most important being that size and strength will forever be determining factors in survival, and I'm heavily lacking in both.

The thought crosses my mind that I could concentrate real hard and probably manage to shift, testing out Fausto's claim about what I am - but even if I did, I wouldn't have the first clue how to fight in anything other than the form I've got right now.   And that's messing with my head, because this werewolf is enormous.

And he's settled into a spot just about eight inches away from the one I'm currently occupying.

"We just want to live over there with the rest of humankind. Because that's what we are, Clarissa.   The Creator made us just the same as he made them."

Them.   He's already put me on his side of the rift and everyone else is the enemy.   He's pushing it into my head that Kaine is the opposition.   That my loyalties are going to have to be with *him*.   The monsters.

The Abominations.

"Don't you think maybe that's something you should take up with him then?   The Creator?"

"You kidding me?   You really think he listens to us?   He never did, that's why he allowed us to be locked up like criminals and freaks in the first place.   We're insults against his perfect species.   We're an annoying fly buzzing around his head."

"Maybe Kaine can - "

"He doesn't listen to Kaine either.   And you're an idiot if you think he's still around or gives a shit about any of us.   I have my doubts whether he's even still alive - and if he is, he's buggered off to some other universe to play with some other species.   This planet's a throwaway, a testing ground, an abandoned experiment, whatever.   He doesn't care what goes on here...we're on our own."

Deep down inside I know there's a lot of truth in what he's saying.   But I'm having a hard time accepting the Maker's part in how it all went bad...a holdout from a childhood spent in the care of a set of highly religious parents, now being challenged by a living, breathing piece of evidence that yeah, maybe there's a whole other side to it all.

"This world is a petri dish left on the table to grow and multiply however it sees fit, it's uncontrolled and unmanaged but constrained by the limits of the dish.   Arbitrary and outdated rules that were put on us before the scientist walked out and never came back.   Rules like...everything on that side of the rift gets to propagate and keep itself alive with fresh blood while everything on this side grows old and dies off without replacing itself. How is any of that okay, little girl?"

He reaches for me and a training so deeply embedded in me that it's instinct now kicks in, meaning I've stepped back out of his reach and palmed the hilt of something sharp and jagged without a brain cell's worth of thought put into any of it. There's a tense few seconds where he almost looks hurt by my reaction, and then he smiles and a laugh rumbles through the quiet. But it's a derisive laugh, and I realize he was only going to touch my face. An affectionate gesture from a werewolf...not something I thought I would ever see in my lifetime.

"Never forget where we came from, Clarissa. No matter where we all end up after today...remember that we were born in the light and we're as entitled to it as anyone."

All I can do is nod. There's no argument I can dig my heels into, no corner I can defend that's justifiable in the face of this. Fausto is right. Monsters weren't made, they weren't created by someone whose intention was to build something twisted. They came into being, naturally. Maybe it wasn't supposed to happen that way and someone broke the rules at the very beginning and started the snowball rolling down the hill, but the end result couldn't be blamed any more than a baby is at fault for being born.

"Kaine's a monster too, you know."   I don't know why I said it, but Fausto's eyebrow shoots up with immediate interest.

"Yeah?   How you figure that?"

"He was born mortal just like everyone else over here.   He committed the first murder after the creation of man.   An eternity of slaying, that was his punishment."

"Fuck.   That was him?"   Recognition brings a smile to his face and he laughs again, a harsh but not entirely unpleasant sound echoing in the silence of the room.   "Well I wouldn't say he totally deserved it, I've heard Abel was an asshole."

"I dunno, he doesn't talk about it.   Took me thirty years to get it out of him."   I wait while Fausto finishes chuckling, then continue with a narrative that somehow seems too important to leave unsaid.   Kaine and Fausto are blood enemies, but in light of all the unvarnished truths being dragged into the bright sun of day, I don't feel like I can keep my opinion to myself.   And my opinion is that both sides have been pitted against each other by a player that grew tired of the game and walked off a long damn time ago.   "He's just doing his job, but I think it's more than that. I think he can't stop.   It's not just a punishment, it's a curse. He *has* to do it."

"Maybe so."   He seems almost pensive for a second, stroking one huge hand down his shaggy beard.   "But

230

he's doing it, and I gotta stop him if I'm gonna bring my people out here where they belong.   That means I have to stop you too.   And that's gonna hurt real bad, little girl."

A lot of things happen in the course of the next few seconds while my head wraps around what my ears just heard.   Aiden steps into the room at the same time the rift opens behind Fausto.   The sudden burst of light, the explosion of the darkness of the Other Side hitting the light of this side, blinds me just long enough for me to lose track of where everyone is and I'm instantly terrified that Aiden will do something stupid and get himself killed before I can refocus my eyes.   And Fausto is still talking, confusing the whole thing even further with words that just keep sending that same jolt of baldfaced fear through my gut over and over.   I've never really felt fear before, but I'm being introduced to it now and it's doing its best to reach out and shake my hand like an old friend I've never actually met.

It's a new feeling that don't like much, because I know where it's coming from.   I'm not afraid of Fausto and I'm not afraid of whatever he's about to do to me.

I'm afraid of what's going to happen to Aiden, and of the fact that there will be nothing I can do to stop it from happening.

"I'm gonna take you back to where you belong until you agree to help us - "

"Aiden, call Kaine."

" - and you're going to realize what you are and accept it, and once you have I'm gonna come back across that line with you beside me. You can be an ally or you can be a human shield, the choice will be entirely yours."

"Now, Aiden."

"And then I'm going to kill your boy over there just to make it stick."

"Get out of here Aiden, now!!"

I don't have time to turn around and see if he's obeying me before Fausto has moved toward me, so quick and smooth that nothing registers until he's got a hand around my throat and is slamming me to the floor. His other hand is gripped in a deathlock around my wrist, pulling my arm back and upwards behind me, and just like that I'm completely, irrefutably, powerless.

And then that giant boot comes down on my shoulder, and I hear two things: the sickening snap of my glenohumeral joint tearing in two, and Aiden screaming from somewhere in the distance.

CHAPTER THIRTY ONE

I know now what Kaine meant all those times he told me it was going to come down to me one day, that I would be the last one standing, that everything would end up balanced on my shoulders. I never knew the truth behind any of it, that I was from both worlds and that he'd taken me for two reasons...I was his personal revenge against Fausto for the death of his wife, and I was insurance for the endtimes he knew would be coming.

Kaine had made sure the world would keep on going the way it always had. As long as one of Fausto's offspring walked this side, the fleshrender would never lead a full on strike against humanity. I was the last of his line and I would be the one to broker peace between the two worlds - or I would be the one to give Fausto the victory he wanted against the dubious heroes that locked him and his kind away.

He didn't care much which way it went, because he'd be unchained either way. And Kaine...Kaine would be free as well. With a victorious peace under his belt, he could retire forever.   With an uprising, he could finally die and be rid of his curse.

He didn't care much which way it went, either.

But I care.   I care a lot, because my kids are on this side and it's where I want to keep them.   They might be part lycan or whatever the hell I am but they deserve to live in the sunlight, without knowledge of the nightmare they're so closely tied to.

The irony and hypocrisy of it doesn't escape me.

Fausto isn't all that interested in them, thank god.   Too much of Kaine in them, which likely would make them uncontrollable.   Humans were gifted with free will and a fierce knowledge that they have it and an even fiercer determination to use it, which makes them less than ideal as pack animals.   But he thinks that being on this side will give his people back their ability to procreate, and because of that I'm valuable to him.   I can get that for him, either through my negotiation clout with Kaine or with my own procreative abilities, however long they hold out on the dark side of the dividing line.   I've been willing to listen to his plans and theories, but this is where I draw my own line.   I refuse to be used as breeding stock.   And so it comes down to this -

War, declared on a world that doesn't know it's coming...with one single tired old slayer standing between an army of monsters and the entirety of humankind.

It won't be a fair fight, though I'm willing to wager Kaine will take out a substantial chunk of them before someone gets a lucky shot in. I don't know where I'll be when it all goes down, but if I have my way I'll be sitting this one out. Because I know now what I only suspected before...that the Othersiders never deserved what they were given, and that Kaine and I have been fighting a battle that never should have started in the first place. We're pawns that were tossed onto the board by a disinterested master, and we got pretty damn far across the playing field before the opposition's king came out of the corner and joined the game.

I'm not so sure anymore that I've been on the right side of the conflict all this time, and for that I don't feel worthy to fight with the Others. I also don't want to fight with Kaine and whatever other slayers are going to be coming out of the dark recesses of history once they figure out what's about to happen. For the first time in my life I'm without a side. It's surprisingly freeing.

And now here we are, I'm not sure how much later because time apparently moves differently on the other side of the rift - and Kaine is standing five feet away from me with Aiden beside him. It's an odd thing to see and I stand next to Fausto blinking hard at the pair of them, partly because it's dark on the other side and I haven't seen the sun in a while...but mostly because *Kaine and Aiden.*

Geezus.

There's a heavy shadow of beard shrouding the lower half of Kaine's face and even heavier shadows under his eyes. He looks like he hasn't slept in a week. His long leather coat is rumpled and I know what little rest he's gotten has been executed with it wadded up under his head for a makeshift pillow, probably on top of the McTier bridge. He's always gone there to think, but I know the real reason is likely less simple than that. The bridge is where he first showed me the world, the *real* world, with all its shadows and dark places and the things that move, just barely, in the corner of your eye when you're not paying attention. It's where he made me his partner and it's where he made me his woman, and if I had to point to a place and say *That was our first home,* that bridge would be it.

I can smell the rain on him.

Kaine's never been a romantic fool...but sometimes he comes damn close to it.

But it's Aiden that shocks me. He doesn't look much better than Kaine sleep-wise, but it's the scar running from his left eyebrow down to the middle of his cheek that makes me gasp. I don't know if he got it trying to stop Fausto from dragging me across the line, but I feel it's a pretty fair assumption that that's exactly where it came from. He hasn't shaved in a while and his hair is tied back in a knot.

He looks like he's aged years since the last time I saw him.

He's staring at me, but Kaine - Kaine has eyes only for Fausto.   Which is pretty telling concerning our relationship, to be honest.   Always professional, always focused on the situation at hand, always trusting me to take care of myself. He's right, of course.   Those icy steel blues should never leave the big werewolf, and despite the fact that I wish for just one brief moment that they would, I'm filled with admiration as always for the man who made me a killer.

But I'm not a killer today, I'm something of an ambassador…and I've got something to say.

"Kaine Carmichael, I'm calling your ass out old man."

Everybody - Fausto included - turns their head toward me with a motley assortment of cocked eyebrows and total befuddlement.   Five Othersiders are standing behind us and I can feel their eyes on me too, hear their heads turn to look at each other.

"Clary, come away from him."

"No, I'm not gonna do that Kaine.   Fausto isn't going to hurt me and you know exactly why.   Now I'm going to say what I have to say and then I'm going to leave you to it. Kill each other if you want, but me and Aiden are walking out of here.   He's not a part of this and now neither am I."

Aiden tilts his head to one side like a confused dog.   I can tell by the whiteknuckle fists he's got clenched at his sides that he's decided to be a soldier for what he no doubt believes to be the righteous side of history. But I know he's just a twenty-nine year old dad to a three year old baby girl, and he's brave because he thinks he has to be.

"The only casualties in here are going to be *you* and *you* - " I jab a finger at Kaine and then at Fausto - "Nobody else. Because Kaine didn't start this and Fausto didn't earn it, and the person responsible for the whole damn thing isn't around to take the blame. And we all know what happens when soldiers go to battle to end fights that other people started."

"Clary, shut up and move out of the way."

I don't know why, but I step in front of Fausto. "Why? You need a clear shot with that ramba you've got shoved up the back of your coat? I can hear it humming from here Kaine, you've put it in hunt mode for someone in this room and I doubt it's me. Or is it?"

"I said *move*."

"And I said no."

"Can I say something?"

Every head turns to Aiden this time. My eyes go to that scar - it's mostly healed and I wonder for the second time just how long I was on the Other Side - and I feel sick to my stomach thinking that he earned it trying to save me. I'm not worth the blood they took from him and I'm certainly not worth the risk he took in shedding it.   But he did it, whatever it was he did, and I can't let it be for nothing.

But I'm about to.

"Aiden you need to leave, this isn't your fight."

He shakes his head, not looking at me.   "Nope, I'm in it, same as you are.   You know why?"

There's a long pause and we all look at each other once it's stretched into the realm of discomfort.   Fausto finally breaks it with an uncertain clearing of his throat.   "No, why?"

"Because I live here.   Right here, on this planet, with all the rest of you.   And if things are gonna go ugly and we're all going to suffer, I want to stand in front of the cause of the problem and at least slow it down before it gets to where my kid is, because even though none of us in here are innocent anymore, she still is."

None of us say anything.   It's a longer, more uncomfortable fog of silence than it was a minute ago, and to the last person we all know Aiden's right.   There's nothing profound or enlightening in what he said, but the simple truth and determination in his words has left us all with nothing better to add to it.

Until Fausto, again, breaks the silence.

"Okay speedbump, if that's how you want it."

239

I hear the *schhhhhickkktt* of a blade leaving its sheath and know everything's about to go very south very fast.   I also know it's Kaine that's armed himself and that it'll be Fausto he goes for, followed by anyone from behind us who dares to step into the fray.   Aiden and I will be casualties unless we join in, and the reality of that contingency is that I'm the only one with half a prayer of coming out of it alive.

"Kaine give him what he wants."

"What?"

"Just do it.   Give him what he wants.   It seems to me you're just about the highest authority on the planet at the moment, so it's not exactly above your pay grade to grant a wish is it?"

"Get out of the way Clary."

"I mean it Kaine, nobody's answering prayers these days, right?   So if He's - " I point to some nondescript place in the sky - "left on vacation and you're the oldest living human, that puts you in charge doesn't it?"

"You know it doesn't."

"Why doesn't it?"

He looks confused for a second and I know I've got him between a rock and a truth that he's never considered. It's a simple truth, but Kaine's never been one to do things the easy way.

"Nobody's in charge down here, not on a cosmic scale. So why not you?   You've been here longest, nobody knows more than you about how things work."   I turn my argument to Aiden on the assumption that he'll be the one out of the pair of them most willing to listen to reason over the drawing of blood.   "You know how when you're a kid and your parents go out, they leave the oldest sibling in charge.   Right?   Why shouldn't the same thing apply here?"

Fausto drags his glare off Kaine just long enough to lay a nasty look on me.   "Who says I gotta agree to that?"

"Why wouldn't you?   All you know is how life is on the Other Side and you want to live out here.   What do you know about being out here?   Kaine is the authority on this side, even you have to acknowledge that."

"Who says Kaine is going to be fair if we take that route?"

It's Aiden, and all eyes shift back to him.   We're starting to look like an old black and white slapstick movie, the crowd's attention constantly ping-ponging back and forth each time someone starts to talk.   But talk is good, and for the first time in my life I'd like nothing better than for everyone to put their weapons down and just yammer for a while.

"Yeah, who's gonna hold him to whatever standard we agree on?"

We all turn around and stare at one of the werekind standing behind Fausto.   Fausto shoots him a *shut up* look, but it's a fair question and this is an equal opportunity war meeting.   And I have the answer.

"We all will."

Kaine is shaking his head in disagreement, disbelief, disgust - pretty much everything prefaced by a dis - and I'm nodding to counteract it all as quick as I can because this, with some fine tuning *this* can work if everyone agrees to it. Both sides have been living by rules made before any of them with the exception of Kaine were ever even born, without question and without real issue.   There have been rebellions and uprisings and the equivalent of kids sneaking out their bedroom windows since the dawn of time, but there's nothing out of the ordinary about any of that.   All in all, the rules have been enforced and obeyed as much as any outfit operating without a boss can expect them to be.

With a new boss, someone actually enforcing the rules as opposed to just punishing the breaking of them like we've been doing all this time, who knows how much more amenable things could be for both sides?

"I'll personally keep him honest."

"So will I."

Kaine glances back, but his eyes are on the floor.   I doubt Aiden's gentle threat in support of mine holds much water

"God gave you your skills and you gave me mine.   Who gave him his?"

There's a moment, just a tiny one, when I'm taken aback by the look on Kaine's face.   He's always hated it when I switch directions on him and I can see him regrouping, trying to figure out a way to sidestep the question.   And then he simply shrugs.   "I don't know."

"Who would know?"

He's walking away from me now with that angry glare on his face that's always just made him more disgustingly handsome.   "Probably no one."

Not good enough.   Not anywhere close to good enough.

"Who's our boss these days, Kaine?"

"Go home woman."

"Is it the Vatican?   The government?   Some shadowy Illuminati organization?   *Lucifer?*"

"I said go home."

"Who's our boss, Kaine."

He keeps going, and right up till the moment he reaches the end of the corridor I believe he's going to walk out without ever giving me an answer.   And I can live with that, it's not like it's something I'm not used to...but we've turned a major corner in both our relationship and the status of our futures and I won't be disrespected by a man who just stood five feet from me and my abductor and never deigned to ask me if I was alright.   That's quite enough of that for me.

"WHO IS OUR FUCKING BOSS?!?"

His hand is on the door, whiteknuckling the crossbar, and when his shoulders slump just slightly I know, I *know* he's going to turn his head just far enough for me to see his eyes but not far enough to actually look at me.   Kaine Carmichael's big dramatic pose, meant to let him keep his self appointed superiority and undisputed authority while simultaneously hiding how lost he actually is when he knows he hasn't got a leg left to stand on.

"I am."

CHAPTER THIRTY THREE

"What the hell do you think you're doing Ubiec?"

Kaine stops - something I'm not expecting, and I walk straight into his back right before Aiden walks into mine. It would be embarrassing if Fitz wasn't standing twenty feet behind us with one hand inside his suit jacket, looking ridiculously men in black-ish and absolutely serious about getting that angry glare of his just right. It doesn't sit well on his stupidly pretty face and we all just stare at him, a bit dumbfounded at what he's doing here. Aiden groans and I have just enough time to wonder if something's happened between them since I've been gone, right before every alarm I've got starts blaring in my head that something very bad is about to go down in this parking lot regardless of the status between my two fellow Suddenly Singles buddies. Because there's a crackling in the air that I've felt before, but only once, and it wasn't a good thing back then - so I can only assume it's not a good thing now either. I try to remember who that slayer was, the one Kaine carefully avoided crossing paths with but still managed to run headlong into that time we got ourselves

hopelessly surrounded by lycans.   Razorfang?   The guy's
colorful name is eluding me, but I haven't forgotten how
the sky lit up and bolts of lightning exploded against the
ground around them when they locked swords that night.
It was like watching the Archangel and Lucifer duke it out
while the elements cheered their favorite from the sidelines.

It crosses my mind that some of the lycans we killed that
night before he showed up might have been my brothers.

But something else is nagging at me and I shove that
unwelcome thought to the back to be dealt with and self-
guilted about later.   What's bothering me now is that left-
hand-across-the-body reach that felt so familiar to me
when I first met Fitz, the one he's doing right now, and I
realize why it set me on edge that day.

Kaine is doing the same exact thing.

So did Venomtongue or whatever his name was, that night
when he and Kaine squared off in the storm.

Definitely the same guy.

That's when I know Fitz is a slayer, just like us.   Maybe he's
not the same person he was back then - he doesn't look
the same, though to be fair I never got a good square look
at the guy and secondlifers sometimes get recycled with
different faces.   Maybe he's purposefully changed his
looks, been promoted to a desk job and hasn't engaged
in any real hand to hand in a few centuries aside from his
tussle with Kaine.   But I have no doubt as he pulls an iron

clad fist back out of his jacket that he remembers how this works.   And then it seeps in, and I'm certain that Fitz was the other participant in that battle.

It's hard not to laugh, because the poor guy tends to lose his head every time he gets near my ex.

"I was just wondering that myself to be honest," Kaine growls, his eyes trained carefully on Fitz's hands.   The left hand, glinting threateningly in the light of the parking lot streetlamp that just flickered on, has his full attention and I know that iron glove's got to be something really badass if he's this nervous about it.   "I came here to shut down some bullshit but it seems there's just more of it now."   That last bit is aimed at me but I've cared far less about far more important things - and right now I'm watching Aiden do the same thing with his left hand that Fitz and Kaine are doing, and it's giving me all kinds of feelings I don't want to be dealing with during a square-off in a library parking lot at dusk.   The look on Aiden's face is saying more than I feel comfortable interpreting.

Fitz looks past Kaine for a second, assessing the threat.

"I still need to know who marked you, Magnussen."

Aiden shrugs, that left hand still inside his coat.   "Told you. There were several of them."

Fitz laughs, squinting against the rapidly falling sun that's behind me and Aiden.   The crackling in the air is getting worse.   "That's a death warrant if it's from Fausto, you know that don't you?   We're not in Miss Hailey Wilcox's knitting circle anymore, there's no coffee intermission while Jeff Porter tries to stop crying about his ex taking the dog. This is the hellfire league and that mark makes it open season on you."

"Like I said, there were several of them.   Fausto had his hands on Clarissa so it must not have been him."

Fitz obviously doesn't believe him.   But the sun is dropping fast and something else is becoming obvious - whoever it was that gave Aiden that scar, they're not the only ones that marked him.

His eyes are starting to glow, an eerie silvery green that I know will show him anything hiding in the dark that doesn't belong there.

Kaine's mark.

Holy shit, that's unexpected.

I'm staring at him when Fitz turns his attention back to Kaine, but I can't pull my eyes off that startling glow in Aiden's soft green irises.   Kaine gave me the mark when I was twenty and then only after I'd earned it.   I can't imagine under what circumstances he would have given it to Aiden, but as the sky dims his eyes just keep getting brighter.   He'll learn to regulate that with time, but for now he looks possessed.

It's oddly arousing.

It's even more oddly arousing thinking about Kaine touching him, holding his head in his hands with his thumbs rubbing across Aiden's eyelids while he whispers those profanely sacred words to transfer a bit of his own countercurse into my lover's eyes. The countercurse that was given to him by his own creator to level the playing field just a little, to allow the first hunter to see his prey in the dark. Most Othersiders have powers that give them the advantage over their human hunters, and Kaine's mark evens the odds.

The disconcerting thought crosses my mind that Kaine is Aiden's creator now, the architect of what I'm looking at in this darkening parking lot. Did he do it out of spite? Was this gift meant to take the innocent thing I used to separate myself from him and corrupt it before he claimed it for himself? Was he intending to replace me on the assumption that I wouldn't be coming back from the other side of the line that Fausto dragged me across? Or had he trained him just enough to give him the confidence he needed to walk into a battle he couldn't possibly walk out of...?

Aiden...geezus, I'm so sorry.

I'm staring hard at him but he's hardly looked at me since we left the library, his eyes are locked to Fitz and Kaine and have only strayed to me briefly before closing tight like he's in pain. For however long I've been gone Kaine has had him, training him for a new reality that I would have sent him away from. He's left his old life and entered a new one. He's a slayer now.

There's a deep and heavy sadness in that, because Aiden is the sweetest person I've ever known. I don't know if he's killed yet, but it's obvious by his behavior this night that he's ready to.

And I'm not ready for that.

"Did you make the deal?"

"What deal?"

Fitz curses under his breath. "Didn't you read the Addendum? You *didn't* read it, did you. Goddamn illiterate thug."

"Last Carmichael standing, yeah I read it."

"Last Carmichael standing at the end. The *end*, Kaine. The end that's coming now that you've gone and given them permission to come out."

Kaine shakes his head. "No, Fausto's going to keep them in line on his side and we'll be watching this side."

"That's not going to be enough. That's not going to be anywhere near enough." Fitz looks up, shaking his head in a despairing sort of resignation that makes my stomach clench up. "There's a new breed of Othersider that's been coming across at other tears in the rift. You haven't seen one yet because they're not native to this end." He points to himself and glares at Kaine. "Why do you think I was assigned here? It wasn't to creep on your wife. I'm watching the damn rift like you should have been doing. Clarissa and that singleshot kid over there are the only ones doing their job these days."

Kaine's eyes flit over to us for just a second, then go right back to that iron fist enveloping Fitz's left hand. Aiden looks at me in confusion. "What's a singleshot?"

"A onelifer. Mortal." I raise my hand and make a gun gesture at his head, pulling the imaginary trigger once. He gets the point.

"You're mortal too, though."

"Not exactly."

His eyebrow goes up and all I can think, oddly, is that the vision in his left eye is likely compromised by that injury he took the day Fausto dragged me across. The scar runs vertically down his eyelid, there's no way he didn't lose at least some of his sight to the blade sharp claws that ripped

his face open.   At least the night vision will override that
when he's in the dark.   Aiden's a creature of the night
now whether he wants to be or not, and damn if that
doesn't break my heart right in half.

"What kind of new breed?"

Fitz takes a step toward us and it's not the least bit
nonthreatening.   Aiden steps in front of me at the same
time Kaine steps in front of him.   Fitz pauses and looks at
each of us in turn, but it's not hesitation that makes him
stop where he's standing.   I can see it now.   Handsome
Mr Not Bad Earnest is a cold blooded killer and he's got no
compunction about taking us all on if he has to.   The
unmistakable chill in his deepset blue eyes says clearly that
he doesn't care if it's one at a time or all at once.   "You're
gonna find out.   They're going to start swarming and
whatever delusions you've got about retirement are going
down the toilet.   Get ready, Ubiec."

"I'm ready, čerep bludnik.   Are you?"

Three things happen in rapidfire succession.   First, my head
latches onto the translations of what they're calling each
other.   It's ancient Macedonian, and though I don't speak
it I've heard enough of it over the years when Kaine is mad
to know these words in particular.   Fitz is calling Kaine *killer*
and Kaine is calling Fitz - loosely rendered - *skullfucker*.
Yeah, the well groomed and immaculately attractive
blonde man in front of us definitely isn't a newly divorced
accountant if he's managed to reap that sort of a

nickname for himself.   And the two of them most definitely are no longer discussing the likelihood of an invasion and have moved right along to calling each other out, because apparently that's what ancient buddies-turned-immortal-enemies do on Wednesday evenings.

Which excites me right down to my sensible beige underwear, because I *really* want to see both of them get their asses kicked.   I've got a sneaking suspicion that Fitz is someone else, someone distinctly biblical, and that his beef with Kaine has more to do with that first murder outside the gates of Eden than a personal disagreement between the two of them.   The sanctuary cities never officially lost their status and it's always been a mystery why Kaine is so attached to Van Alta.

The second thing that happens is Kaine whips out a half-blade sword that I recognize as one of the venom edged weapons he pilfered from a Rosicrucean cathedral sometime in the fifth century.   It's a legendary blade, able to kill with just a superficial scratch if the bearer wishes it. Fitz's eyes go to it and he grins.   "So that's where those went."

"It was either me or they went home with a shadow troll." Kaine points the blade toward Fitz's hand while moving into an attack position away from me and Aiden.   "You're one to talk, wearing the Fist of Mephisto.   Isn't that supposed to be locked up in a vault seven miles under the Sahara?"

"Why don't you save some syllables and just call it Mefisto?"

They've obviously forgotten Aiden is standing ten feet from them and his voice startles them - and when they both turn to look at him, the third thing happens.

"Not here!"

Everyone including me is taken by surprise because that voice doesn't belong to anyone present; Aiden nearly comes out of his skin and his hand goes straight to the back of his jeans where I know he's got at least one weapon stashed, maybe two.   I feel sick for a second at the thought of him being hardcore conditioned to the point where his first reaction is to arm up instead of a good sensible duck and dive.   The difference between my training and Kaine's - I taught him to back up, use his head, be ready but wait as long as possible before going on the offensive.   Kaine's method is the exact opposite, and it's clear it's overridden mine.   Which really sends a jolt of dreadful reality through my gut, because when I first met him not so terribly long ago Aiden held a kitchen knife with such uncertainty that it was a shock he ever managed to slice a tomato.   Now he's ready to bring out a blade against a human being.

A human being that runs the Research and Genealogy departments inside the library we're getting ready to brawl outside of.   Marta is standing on the steps with her hands on her hips and the mildly annoyed look of a kindergarten teacher shushing a classroom full of rowdy five year olds anxious for recess. I figure that's about as close as Marta can get to actual anger.

"Go back inside, girl." It's Kaine, growling and misogynistic as always, and Marta gets her back up good and righteous because god help her we're standing on her territory and no man is going to boss her outside a building where her degrees are hanging.

"No! You're not going to fight here, the seven o'clock knitting group is going to be arriving any minute and I think they're going to notice a bunch of assholes waving their *cosas puntiagudas* around in the parking lot!"

"What's casa ponygouda?"

Aiden shrugs. "I dunno. Dicks maybe?"

Marta is waving her hands now, flustered and speaking so fast in Spanish that none of us can follow her. "Puntiagudo!" She points at Kaine's sword. "Pointy things!"

I nod at Aiden. "Yeah, she means dicks."

"Take it in the backside!"

Fitz squints at her and Kaine cocks his head to one side. It takes a bit of wild gesticulation before she finally makes her point clear - she wants us to relocate the battle to the alley behind the library. Where we currently are is shielded from view of the street by a carefully cultivated hedgerow, but she's right, it's Knotty Knitters night in the community room and I for one don't feel like having to defend myself from a bunch of vigilante housewives with long needles once they realize there's untoward activity taking place outside their venue.

But since Kaine and Fitz don't seem willing to do much more than stand there staring at each other like a couple of pit bulls in the dog park defending a patch of grass they've both decided is theirs, I give Aiden a hard smack on the shoulder and tell him it's time for him to get lost.

"Go home pretty boy, this doesn't concern you and there's about to be a storm.   Don't want your hair getting frizzy."

He doesn't move.   Surprising, considering how hard I hit him.   Before I crossed the rift that punch would have sent him staggering back a couple of steps.

"No way, I want to see this."

"Yeah?"

"Yeah."   There's a look of the devil about him as he shoves a hand into the pocket of his jeans and pulls out a wadded up bill.   "I got twenty on a draw.   And you were gone for six months."

"Was I?"   There's a shocker - I know time runs different once you cross the line but I had no idea it was that big of a shift.   It felt like a few days, maybe a week.   There's a second of panic when I realize my kids have been with Kaine and Kaine's been neck deep in getting ready for armgeddon, but odds are good he's shipped them off to my parents for the duration.   Probably told them mom had a breakdown and needed some alone time. "Geezus...did you miss me?"

The sideways look he levels on me comes damn near close to shaking me to my bones.   There's a lot of confusion in that look, peppered with a healthy dose of anger and regret and a dash of longing that might not actually belong there.   "Yeah, I missed you.   Kinda thought you were dead.   Kaine though...he just kept saying to wait."

Figures.   Kaine's first, second, and third assumptions are always to just take for granted that I'm alive and reasonably well, and that if I need help I'll make it known. Non-survival, regardless of the circumstances, would be his very last assumption.

You're alive until I see a corpse he'd told me the first time we got separated in a battle.   I was spitting mad when I finally found him a half mile away, cleaning black blood off his boots with a complete lack of concern for my current status and zero interest in finding out what I'd just done to walk out breathing without his help.   Of course he would tell Aiden to just wait.   No corpse, no worry.

"I wanted to come get you, Clarissa.   I want you to know that.   Kaine wouldn't let me."

There's nothing but truth on his face.   It's unsettling and I don't want to address it, acknowledge it, or otherwise let on that it's affecting me as deeply as it is, so in lieu of having actual emotions I reach out and snatch the crumpled twenty from his hand.

"I'll take that.   My money's on a beheading."

We watch as Kaine and Fitz trudge toward the side of the building, still holding their weapons out in the open like two immortal badasses who honestly don't care what the regular humans see.   Nobody would believe it anyway, mortals tend to write off anything that doesn't fit neatly into the assortment of little boxes they like to tuck normal life into.   And though I hate that Kaine trained some of his own steeliness into Aiden's soft heart while I was away, there's something less resentful tugging at my new view of the tall, gangly, sweet faced hippie boy that just weeks ago was falling asleep during group and getting his feelings hurt over my codependance with the world's most intimidating ex husband.   It's something disturbingly like a guilty pride in the fact that Aiden Magnussen, computer arts assistant professor at Van Alta Junior College and weekend stoner, is now a warrior.   Maybe a junior warrior...a little shaky, a lot nervous, but willing and ready and operating on reflex as much as coherent thought. Kaine must have recruited him the minute I disappeared because slayer skills, even beginning ones like that, don't come over the course of a weekend.

At least he didn't take my absence as permission to kill him and dump him in a ditch somewhere.

Sometimes you take small blessings wherever they turn up.

CHAPTER THIRTY FOUR

The storm is starting by the time we make it to the back of the library. Lightning is flashing directly over the alley courtyard in an isolated outburst that the weather channel is going to have a hard time explaining, but at least there are no standard humans hanging around at this hour to question any of it. Except Aiden, and he's not asking. It's an odd thing, realizing there's only one full human mortal in your group and it isn't you. Sort of like it's an odd thing watching the elements cheer their favorite side of a street brawl between two demimorts that technically shouldn't exist.

Kaine and Fitz are already at it and blood has been drawn - a deep diagonal gash over Kaine's right eye from scalp to brow that isn't slowing him down in the least. Fitz has a knife in one hand and that cursed iron fist on the other and he's advancing so fast that Kaine has no choice but to back up, but the moment the heel of his boot hits the alley wall he spins around and plants one foot against the bricks and launches himself. It's impressive, and in the half heartbeat between getting airborne and landing so close to Fitz that they could kiss if they were so inclined, a violent flash of lightning hits the building.   Aiden and I watch it travel along the rain gutter, both of us fully aware of where it's going.

If a higher power hasn't been watching all this time, there's sure as hell one tuning in now.

The bolt of pure electricity takes out the transformer on the pole behind us at the same exact moment the library is illuminated in the brightest blast of light I've seen since Kaine threw a flash grenade into a riftwitch bonfire during the '87 uprising.   And then it all goes dark, and all we can see until our eyes adjust is the unearthly spectre of sparks flying as metal hits metal in the blackened courtyard while two cursed souls take their eternal frustrations out on each other's corporeal forms.

When Fausto steps out of the library he squints for a second, face turned up to the sky, before he raises his gigantic arms and turns them palm up.

It's raining and he's smiling.   It's obviously been a long time since he's felt rain on his skin or smelled the air outside of the library.   The crack in the rift - the Genealogy section - has pretty much been the extent of his freedom range, the restrainer branded into the skin on the side of his thick neck keeping him from going any further than the door. But he's free now, thanks to that maybe not so stray bolt of lightning that shut off everything inside the building with the deafening sound of Zeus cracking a whip.   Looks like it killed more than just the electricity.

"It's night," he says with a gentle sort of exasperation. "Figures."

And then he looks at me and Aiden, and the hesitation that softens his rough face is more of a question than if he's opened his mouth and asked.

We good?

I don't expect Aiden to give his blessing.   I don't expect him to even acknowledge Fausto directly, much less nod his head and offer up a tired little smile in response.   But he does, and when I reach over to touch his arm I can feel him trembling inside his coat.   Could be a quiet rage, could be fear, could be the bone shaking dread that comes with the cursed knowledge of things that are probably on their way as a direct result of someone else's sins.   Or it could just be the chilly bite of oncoming winter in the night air getting inside him because he's so damn skinny.   Whatever it is, it's got a hard hold on him and he turns away, pulling his arm out of my grip and heading off across the alley toward the street while Fitz and Kaine just keep battling in the courtyard behind us, oblivious to everything but their grudge match with each other.

CHAPTER THIRTY FIVE

So that's how we averted the oncoming apocalypse, with an adult conversation and a quiet nod of approval while a schoolyard asskicking - most definitely *not* the one we were expecting - played out in the background.   The first wave of Othersiders have come across, blinking in the bright sunlight that I'm sure feels like the kiss of heaven on their shadowed skin.   It's a tentative exploration and they're free to go back if they find it doesn't suit them.   There's just one rule - everybody behaves or everybody goes back, and the minute somebody breaks that rule Kaine and I come right back out of retirement.   Both sides know there's going to be growing pains and mistakes, but there can't be any tolerance in the mix.   We're allowing creatures with checkered pasts - vampires and werewolves and all manner of storied monster - to assimilate into a culture of humanity that has a fear of things that go bump in the night.

There will be problems, we all know it.   And the first time the evening news flashes a report about mutilated cows in Ohio or a rash of bitten necks in New York, a small handful of us will be on it.   The Other Side has agreed to do their best to keep their folks toeing the line, but the fact remains that it's us that have drawn that line.   It won't agree with everyone.

Fausto has gone back across in a personal choice to remain behind, guiding his people as they sort out how to integrate slowly into life on this side.   He'll come back across when all who want to come have come.   I don't think he's ready, honestly.   A classic case of wanting something so badly that you never stop to think if it's the right thing for you.   Fausto is a leader, a strong voice breaking up the darkness, a presence that all eyes turn to for the strength they can't possess on their own.   Nothing comes to mind when I try to think of what he would do on this side.   But sometimes I think I see him, late at night when the only light is the city's sparkly glow and the headlights of passing cars.   He doesn't try to interact with me, though I honestly wouldn't mind if he did.   There's a whole history there that I don't have, a history that he can fill in the blanks to.   I don't feel any different in general, but every time I catch a glimpse of him in the shadows, I have just a little bit of an urge to howl at the moon.

Nobody knows who won the testosterone spewing match between Fitz and Kaine that night.   I've still got Aiden's twenty but he hasn't missed it yet.   There was a segment on the news the next night about weird meteorological events isolated over small parts of the city, with a short clip of Marta being interviewed by the local station about the lightning strike at the library.   There was so much excited ranting in skewered Spanish that most of what she said was unintelligible, and then she lapsed back into English just long enough to confirm that yes, lightning took out the library's electricity and it was *muy loud* and the Knotty Knitters group was *very* disappointed because they were supposed to learn how to pearl that night.

Bless her.

Life and time and the natural progression of both have continued trudging along, dragging us all with them. Kaine has apologized to Fitz for all the ignominious beheadings he's subjected the poor man to over the years, though I don't really think their friendship or their partnership will be rekindling any time this century and I'm not the least bit convinced the apology was sincere or that it will stick. Kaine is officially an outlaw now after breaking his sacred edict to keep the Othersiders off our lawn, and technically Fitz is supposed to be tracking him down and eliminating him. His other, newer job is keeping him too busy to bother though, watching over things with this side's new tenants, keeping an eye out in case shit goes messy. And it will. He knows it, I know it, Kaine knows it. The Othersiders know it. And so an uneasy truce is forged between all the creatures that are now sharing space on this side, and Colin Fitzpatrick is a god among men as he walks the daylight and the dark both, doing what time and destiny have decreed for him. He halfheartedly hunts

Kaine when he's bored of maintaining law and order and the two of them play their little game of Avenger and Condemned, setting the back streets of Van Alta on fire with their little slap matches but never really managing to do each other much damage - although one night about a month into the assimilation he fell off the radar for a few days, and Kaine showed up at my house in an unusually cheerful mood - albeit with the exceptionally conspicuous shape of a hand around his throat in a lovely bruised shade of purple. I didn't ask. But the next time I saw Fitz he looked just a little bit different, like a copy of himself that wasn't quite exact in the details. His hand went to his neck when he saw me. No iron fist, but his glasses seemed to be just a tiny bit thicker than the last time we crossed paths.

Good old Kaine. Fitz insists it was his tenth failed attempt to avenge Abel, a little detail I was apparently correct about; Kaine holds out that it was lucky number seven. The truth, I'm sure, lies somewhere in between - just like it always does.

I don't know if we really are alone in the world, left to figure it all out on our own without any higher power to nudge us in the right direction when we start to lose track of the chalk line we're stumbling across in bemused confusion, navigating life and history and the future with a nervous sort of bravado and blind leaps of faith on the bits where the chalk has blown away in the wind or been rained out of existence.   I don't even know if thinking that way is an unforgivable blasphemy or just the way things are, take it or leave it, with no consequences.   I'd like to think we're not entirely left to our own devices, but until someone steps up and says one way or the other, I've decided to just do my best.   It's all any of us can do in the end.

And the end very well might be coming, for all any of us know.   Not to get all apocalyptically dark but I know my solution to the Othersider issue isn't infallible.   It might just be the least infallible thing any resident of this planet has ever thought up, but here it is, put into play and kicked into action and dragging all of us along with it whether we want to go or not.   There are going to be rulebreakers. There are going to be rebellions.   There are going to be laws ignored and atrocities committed in the name of newfound freedom and liberties will be taken, sneakily if possible, violently if necessary.   But I have faith that there will also be peaceful assimilation and willing cohabitation and, maybe, a bit of acceptance and tolerance in the end.   Because that's what humans hold as their ideal, isn't it?   Peaceful cohabitation, however they can get it.

I know sometimes it's bloody uprising that gives it to us.

I also know that sometimes bloody uprising is for another purpose entirely, and when that happens, Kaine and I will be on it like we always have.

Goddamn Kaine.   The old slayer got one over on his Creator in the end.   His curse was to live until he'd rid Earth of its abominations, but instead he'd played an integral part in clearing the way for them to live in the sunlight again.   Whether he'd actually intended for it to go that way would probably remain a mystery until he finally gave up the ghost, but the world could live with one more unanswered question.   And Kaine would have to go on living in a world that would never know how much he'd done for it.   An eternally bound slayer, turning his back on his holy assignation and demoting himself from avenger to the equivalent of mall cop after all those endless centuries of keeping this side safe.   It was a big step down for him, one that I'm not entirely convinced he'll be content with. But he hasn't dropped dead yet of unknown causes and he hasn't vanished into dust, so the only acceptable conclusion is that he's right.   He is the boss.   I wonder sometimes if he's known all along that there was no one above him, if maybe he knew the exact moment when the higher power packed up and left on eternal vacation.   If he was aware of it he never let on.

And if he's aware of how proud I am of him, he's never let on about that either.

Somehow I don't think he cares too much about that.

CHAPTER THIRTY SIX

Life moves along at its own pace I suppose, no matter how colossally a small handful of its subscribers mess up. Because in the end that's what we are, isn't it?   Lifetime subscribers, always paying our yearly dues until one day it up and expires on us.   Some of us, like Kaine, keep threatening to cancel but find reasons not to right before the deadline.   Others, like me, stay signed up for the long haul with a lifetime sub.   And then there's people like Aiden, staring in confusion at their receipt and wondering if they ordered the wrong one.

So far we're all still here.   Hanging in there, sorting things out, figuring out what we're meant to do now that the apocalypse has been averted and our skillsets are no longer in demand.   It's a disconcerting place to be sometimes, and there are days when I feel like I'm just wandering around looking for a thrill, some danger to bring back the excitement of my slayer days.   I wonder how Kaine is holding up.   The last I heard from him he was somewhere on the Ivory Coast, looking for his brother's grave I suspect.

Some amends shouldn't be left unmade for too long.

Aiden and I quit the Suddenly Singles group. Neither of us feels the need to come to terms with our uncoupled status now that we've both seen things that made us realize our messy little lives aren't nearly as messed up as they could be. He's teaching full time at the university now, still computer sciences, but he's moonlighting on the side teaching a class in archeology that has almost brought back the smile he lost somewhere along the way. I'm happy for him. He says he's still glad he met me and that we sort of saved the world together, but I know if there was a button he could push to wake up and have it all be a whack dream, he'd probably smack that sucker hard enough to break the bedside table.

Or not. Because sometimes he brings his little girl over for ice cream with me and the boys and I can tell he misses it, the rush of excitement that hits you when you're looking at something that shouldn't exist. The thrilling jolt of nervous electricity when you do something you didn't know you could do in a situation you never thought for a second you'd find yourself in. And it's then, as he's sitting across the table from me and I'm staring at the scar that barely misses the center of his eye, that I know without any doubt the second one of the newly arrived Othersiders steps out of line he'll be at my side, ready to go. I know Kaine spent a good chunk of the time I was gone training him, teaching him the basic skills he'll need to survive what might be coming. The skills he'll need to stand with us, if he chooses to. I see it in the new strength clinging to his gangly body, in the thickness to his upper arms and chest that wasn't there the last time I touched him. It's in the deadly flicker of readiness that I sometimes see in his soft green eyes, eyes that maybe aren't quite as soft as they used to be back when he was just a newly divorced young dad fulfilling a court ordered self help program so he could keep seeing his little girl on weekends.

He's come so far, and it's a trip I wish he hadn't had to take down a road so bumpy it's obviously rattled something loose, like that odd squeak coming from somewhere in the vicinity of a car's dashboard that you can never quite figure out the location of. It drives you nuts at first, but eventually you get used to it. Sooner or later you start to associate that little squeak with your car, and the day it doesn't assault your ears is the day you wonder if you got in the wrong one.

But life is like that, isn't it? Nothing stays the same, it's always changing, morphing, destabilizing and reshaping itself into new things, different things, things we may not like but that the universe gives us no say in. And we accept it and just keep going. We keep going and we keep finding ways to survive and love and be happy and, sometimes, just exist. Our little gang might be in a sort of limbo at the moment without any clear indication of where it'll be going in the future, but we know at least that our existence matters...and for me and Aiden, that feels really important.

That's where we are right now, standing in the doorway of the Genealogy section in the Van Alta library, staring at an open rift.

Aiden is holding my hand, and for some reason that makes me smile.

Clarissa, Aiden, and Kaine will return in Book Two

The Magnussen Ultimatum

Thanks to Alana for suffering through late night Google Docs, unexpected character changes, endless writing related neuroses and the inevitable 3pm "tell me how bad this idea sucks" texts from the doctors office waiting room, and for following me through a twisted labyrinth of ludicrous plot shifts and random celebrity crushes. You did me a solid and I won't forget it. Clear your calendar, we're doing it all again on book two.

Thank you to Andrew Hozier-Byrne for being my final physical inspiration for Aiden. You were a last minute substitution but you fell into the character like it was written for you from page one. Book two will be all you all the way, baby. And bless you for the music that kept me writing until the wee hours every night, Moment's Silence will forever be Aiden and Clarissa's anthem.

I'd thank my kids but they're the reason this book is late.

Cover art from an original painting by Lexa Kline

SNEAK PREVIEW

The war, when it came - and it came fast - was big. Much bigger than any of us expected, and by the time it went full blown we were already separated, isolated, alone. Kaine was in Africa. Aiden had vanished to god only knows where. I was still in Van Alta, keeping a lid on the library.

But the library wasn't where they came across this time, and by the time Fitz and I noticed the upswing in paranormal activity it was already too late.

They were here.

- Excerpt from The Magnussen Ultimatum, Book 2 of the Carmichael Trilogy - COMING SOON

Made in the USA
Las Vegas, NV
16 December 2022

62888044R00157